PRAISE F

M000213450

'This is not a novel in which anything catastrophically, and the condition of exile is the only place from which one can achieve peace or perspective. This is what I think this marvellous book is telling us.' – Nick Lezard, *Guardian*

'A dense but rewarding series of W.G. Sebald-like meditations on ideas of belonging.' – David Mills, *The Sunday Times*

'Some literature defies simple description. Case in point, *Panorama*, by Slovenian poet and writer Dušan Šarotar. One might be inclined to define it as a meditation within a travelogue within a novel. Or perhaps you would prefer to rearrange those terms, it probably wouldn't matter, because in spite of its subtitle – *A Narrative About the Course of Events* – *Panorama* stands at a curious angle to space and time. It is a novel of remembering, of telling and retelling, narratives within narratives, bound together by a coarse thread of repeating themes that are at once timeless and timely.' – Joseph Schreiber, *Numéro Cinq*

'This book is about a lot of things. Like all good novels, it is about language . . . It is also about exile and identity and belonging (and not belonging). Of course, it is also about war and death and the terrible upheaval that war causes. It is about the dark side of life, for there is always a dark side. But it is also about friendship and remembrance and learning about the world.' – *The Modern Novel*

'While Šarotar (and his narrator) serve as the mouthpiece for the various émigrés who show up in *Panorama*, Šarotar, who still lives in Slovenia and writes in Slovene, does not seem to share the émigrés' preoccupation with the loss of their birth languages. His ultimate goal is an attempt to capture in a grand, sweeping gesture of language the ineffable sense of being alive, of finding oneself human on a strange planet. It's both a search for personal understanding and an attempt to test the limits of language.' – Terry Pitts, *Vertigo*

'A meditation on loss and change . . . and on time, migration, language, ocean, love and war. It is densely compacted: its two hundred or so pages seem to expand much as a paper flower from childhood did when put in water.' – Stephen Watts, poet and editor, from the 'Afterword' of *Panorama*

DUŠAN ŠAROTAR (b. 1968) is a novelist, poet, playwright and screenwriter. He studied the sociology of culture and philosophy at the University of Ljubljana. To date, Šarotar has published four novels (*Island of the Dead*, 1999, *Billiards at Hotel Dobray*, 2007, *Stay with Me, My Dear*, 2011 and *Panorama*, 2014), three collections of short stories (*Blind Spot*, 2002, *Bed and Breakfast*, 2003 and *Nostalgia*, 2010), three poetry collections (*Feel for the Wind*, 2004, *Landscape in a Minor Key*, 2006 and *The House of My Son*, 2009) and a book of essays (*Neither Sea Nor Earth*, 2012). He was twice shortlisted for the Best Slovene Novel award, and selected works have been translated into Hungarian, Russian, Spanish, Polish, Italian, Czech and English. Šarotar is also the author of fifteen screenplays for documentary and feature films and has taken part in several photographic exhibitions both in Slovenia and abroad.

RAWLEY GRAU, originally from Baltimore, has lived in Ljubljana since 2001. His translations from Slovene include prose works by Vlado Žabot and Boris Pintar, a play by Ivan Cankar and essays by Aleš Debeljak as well as poetry by Miljana Cunta, Janez Ramoveš, Andrej Rozman Roza and others. He has also translated (from Russian), co-edited and annotated the book *A Science Not for the Earth: Selected Poems and Letters* by the nineteenth-century poet Yevgeny Baratynsky. His translation of *Dry Season* by Gabriela Babnik – winner of the EU Prize for Literature 2013 – was published in 2015 by Istros Books.

OTHER TITLES IN
THE WORLD SERIES
SLOVENIAN SEASON

Evald Flisar, *Three Loves, One Death* (translated by David Limon)
Jela Krečič, *None Like Her* (translated by Olivia Hellewell)

PETER OWEN WORLD SERIES
'*The world is a book, and those who do not travel read only one page*,' wrote
St Augustine. Journey with us to explore outstanding contemporary literature
translated into English for the first time. Read a single book in each season
– which will focus on a different country or region every time – or try all
three and experience the range and diversity to be found in contemporary
literature from across the globe.

Read the world – three books at a time

3 works of literature in
2 seasons each year from
1 country each season

For information on forthcoming seasons go to www.peterowen.com.

PANORAMA

Dušan Šarotar

PANORAMA

A narrative about the course of events

Translated from the Slovene by Rawley Grau

PETER OWEN
WORLD SERIES

WORLD SERIES SEASON 1: SLOVENIA

THE WORLD SERIES IS A JOINT INITIATIVE BETWEEN
PETER OWEN PUBLISHERS AND ISTROS BOOKS

Peter Owen Publishers/Istros Books
Conway Hall, 25 Red Lion Square, London WC1R 4RL, UK

Peter Owen and Istros Books are distributed in the USA and Canada by
Independent Publishers Group/Trafalgar Square
814 North Franklin Street, Chicago, IL 60610, USA

Originally published in Slovene as *Panorama* by Beletrina Academic Press
First English language edition published by Peter Owen/Istros Books 2016
(in collaboration with Beletrina Academic Press); reprinted 2017

Editor: Stephen Watts

Paperback ISBN   978-0-7206-1922-5
Epub ISBN   978-0-7206-1923-2
Mobipocket ISBN   978-0-7206-1924-9
PDF ISBN   978-0-7206-1925-6

A catalogue record for this book is available from the British Library.

Printed and bound in Great Britain by
CPI Group (UK) Ltd, Croydon, CR0 4YY

This book is part of the EU co-funded project 'Stories that Can Change the World'
in partnership with Beletrina Academic Press | www.beletrina.si

Co-funded by the
Creative Europe Programme
of the European Union

The European Commission support for the production of this publication does not constitute an
endorsement of the contents which reflects the views only of the authors, and the Commission cannot
be held responsible for any use which may be made of the information contained therein.

For Brigita

It is like a man who has left his home and gone on a journey.

– Mark 13:34

PANORAMA

The wind was blowing low above the sea, in the direction of the house I moved into this morning. I was resting on a low two-seat sofa, a fleece blanket over my knees, and listening to the strange sounds the wind was thrusting about, as if words, the creaking of hinges and the rattling of glass in lonely houses in the dark on distant islands had hidden themselves in pockets of the storm and here, in front of the window through which I watched this imagined sea, had tumbled out over the floor. Words were rolling like multi-coloured marbles, the glass eyes scurrying away, hiding beneath the table, ducking out of sight for a moment as if waiting for inspiration, then taking off again; I felt that maybe if I could freeze them, at least

for a second, could read their placement in the room, I'd be able to capture the thought, the long sentence that was both hiding and revealing itself to me in seemingly random images. It was cold in the room; it will be a while before I get warm, I thought, although the electric radiator was making popping noises as if a fire burned inside it. The orange light that flickered in the decorative stove beneath the black television helped alleviate the sense of false warmth, and every so often, when I opened my eyes and wrenched myself from my musings, I would bring my dry hands closer to the silent stove in the hope that the artificial logs were at last radiating heat and I could at least get warm in my soul, but it was no good. Then I would go back to staring absently out of the window, looking across the road at the grey surface of the water fissured with low, sharp waves, as a young heir might gaze at a blackened seascape by an unknown or forgotten master in which, after long perusal, when he has internalized the picture and believes it holds nothing more to excite him, he suddenly discovers something that fascinates him utterly, maybe even shocks him, as if in this old maritime genre painting, which has hung on the wall since before he was born – placed there, he assumes, by his grand- father – he suddenly recognizes himself. He is sitting in a long coat, alone in the storm on the black rocky shore; in the distance, a light flashing from a lighthouse is refracted in the rainy fog, while terrible fiery branches of lightning strike at the sea on the darkening horizon; at the golden section point, as if on the point of a knife, a heavy ship hovers in the air, which the observer from the shore can only sense, or maybe he has glimpsed it in the dark nebulous stain, the veiled gleam of the clouds, above which rest the moon and thousands of cold stars, which are the only things shining above the romantic seascape, like a miracle in which we see only one thing. The narrow strip of coast that was visible from my third-floor room, from the Galway Business School to the guesthouse, was already completely black; not even the waves rising like ashes into the sky could drive the joggers in their shorts and wind-puffed anoraks from the seaside promenade, nor were the strollers with their long-haired dogs, which were barking and rummaging on strained leashes for washed-away evidence of the morning walk, taking shelter from the storm. Thick raindrops, or maybe it was the sea preparing for a second universal deluge, were washing, were streaming, down the windows; I couldn't tell any more which direction the sharp, swift wind was blasting from; I felt it entering through the crevices in the window sashes, whistling in the keyholes, the walls getting damp; nothing was flying through the air any more – papers, dog barks, birds, sand, cigarette butts, words, anything that wasn't tied down or rooted in the ground the wind had long ago blown away, scattered or smothered like lies. Beneath a high, rocking, yellowish lamp, which stood alone next to the road like the mast of a sinking ship and gave off a light that no longer reached the ground but was washed away by the rain and extinguished by the wind, the last maddened dogs and drenched, lost joggers were still running, despite the sky having warned them hours before, for the love of god, not to risk their bodies tonight to the mercy of the sky and the durability of their hearts. An exodus, I thought, but I myself will stay here cradling my unfinished manuscript and my longing for home in my lap, cast on the turbulent sea – when the light in the silent hearth went out, too; that's when I first made my vow, for who is the only one able to put out the light of a person lost in icy waves, who

can give birth to a word and bestow it on the writer, who accepts it gratefully and in peace and quiet and concentration shapes it into thought and beauty for us all? – that's what I was thinking when I vowed for a second time to describe all of this one day; then, for one last time, before the world and solitude, I vowed out loud, as the wind was tearing the bathroom window from its hinges and the rain was pouring in on the parquet floor in the hall, to write it all down, just as it was and nothing else, the way it had to happen, not according to my will and our will, if I remain on dry land this night. I will remember this night, I will always think of everyone I care for, I will repeat their names like a castaway, just as I do now in this terrible hour, I will not forget, I will remember, with the same ardour and delight with which I gladly remember what is beautiful and good, I kept on repeating until I sank into sleep. I was dreaming, or maybe was already awake, I'm not sure, when, conscientiously and devotedly, I set about fulfilling my vow, in a manner such as only the most ardent perform their service. It was still raining in the morning, sparse raindrops hovering and spinning in the translucent fog that stretched across the bleak Atlantic. I walked along the shore, neither strolling nor jogging, with a determined but slow step; I was hunched over, leaning forward, as if struggling against the wind or some unknown force that was pushing me back; I pressed on, more for the sake of the view that opened and offered itself to me on every side, although now, when I give it some thought, neither at the time nor now can I see anything but the sea – a rolling, windy sea of indefinable hue, neither brown nor blue, but certainly a different colour from what I know, and also smell, here on the Adriatic; at that early hour, the joggers and dog-walkers were already returning to their homes; it crossed my mind that these were the same refugees I saw leaving the night before, or maybe the exodus had never ended and they were running from their homes, from this drowning world, as their ancestors had once fled the Great Famine, fled on ships, brave mariners transporting them in the hold of fragile half-sinking boats, all of them starving, silent, sick, with big pale eyes that saw, from right where I was standing now with a warm black woollen cap on my head and watching, like those dying passengers on creaking boats, the last lighthouse on the western coast of their now-former homeland. For whoever that day stood on one of the many ships that daily departed these shores, that gave themselves over to icy winds and sharp waves as dangerous as the potato knives that lay in the passengers' empty travel bags and tattered pockets as the only sign, the hope, that their bellies would one day be full again, that person had certainly never returned to see, at least one more time, the pale light at the head of Galway Bay, as I read on a memorial plaque that had recently been placed next to the walkway to the lighthouse, my intended destination that morning, in memory of all the mariners and families who between 1847 and 1853 had crossed the Atlantic to escape famine and death. I read and repeated the names of the hundreds of ships engraved in the stone, kept repeating them, but now, as I write, I don't remember a single one. *Go down to the sea.* The tall stainless steel gate, already losing its silvery sheen from the slow corrosion of sea and salt, was closed that morning,

although I could see a few people walking on the low asphalt causeway that led over the rolling sea to the tiny fortified island where Mutton Light stood, an enormous white lighthouse, the last light of home for the travellers who were leaving for ever, an image still resonating in my thoughts, so I turned away from the locked barrier and set off along the shore in the opposite direction. The man-made causeway with the asphalt road connecting the island to the shore had been created not long before; centuries ago, the lighthouse stood alone in the middle of the sea, as I read on the sign hanging on the gate; until recently, to get to the reef where the lighthouse was, you had to row or sail a boat; now as I moved away from it, the causeway slowly melted into the sea; whenever I turned to take another look at the lighthouse tower, it, too, was shorter and less prominent; after a mile or so, all I could make out in the distance, far from the shore, was the big, black reef, and the waves crashing against it from the open sea, breaking into high white foam and spraying across the lighthouse dome and, even before the next wave rose up, disappearing in the wind like the echoing names of the ships in my memory. I remembered that on my first morning here, when I was going out of the city by car, I had noticed a large, yellowish tower on the shore with lots of concrete platforms for diving into the sea. Right away I had wanted to take a picture of it – it was exciting, bizarre, a structure incongruous with the seascape; only later did I wonder why I was so drawn to the diving tower the first time I saw it; maybe somewhere deep in my memory, like a silent, sleeping image I had been guarding since childhood, something had stirred, something I associated with an image from my Saturday swimming club, where exactly the same sort of concrete diving tower, which I used to dive from in terror, had stood above the Olympic swimming pool; similarly, the mighty concrete colossus I saw from the car that day seemed unusually large and tall to me, which, I thought, must mean that at high tide the sea is deep enough for diving; I would like to see that – even though now, as I walked along the shore, I was wearing a woollen cap and lined windcheater; Gjini, the driver and occasional tour guide who had driven me from the city that first morning, had told me that people bathe in the sea year round here, regardless of water temperature or weather. At the time I did not have a chance to take any photos because we were in a hurry – the forecast wasn't good: occasional downpours with thunder, if I correctly understood the prediction on the radio, but I couldn't envisage it, what that looked like here, since it was my first time in this country; now the morning was bright and clear after terrifying wind and rain the whole night, as if I had arrived at the end of the world – which had been my first impression the night before the car trip, when I stepped out of the airport terminal, where Gjini was waiting to drive me to the Hotel Meyrick.

I remembered that the next morning Gjini, wanting to give me a brief introduction to the local sights we drove past, had mentioned the Aquarium, a big glass semicircular building where big, terrible sea creatures were on display – I was passing it now on foot – and that was when, from the car, I first caught sight of the old, enormous yellow pier with the diving platforms, just as I did now. I crossed the road and started running towards my goal. Amazingly, at that very moment the sun came out from behind some high, scattered clouds and lit up the seemingly abandoned municipal bathing site. Just beside the road, beneath the concrete pillars which the sea had been gnawing at, washing away their once-red plaster with decorative yellow stripes, which were still visible on the shady side, were the changing rooms: no cubicles, doors or

partitions, just hooks protruding from the wall, with trousers and shirts hanging on them, and beneath a bare concrete bench men's and women's shoes were arranged, socks folded neatly inside them; maybe the clothes had been left behind, I thought when I saw the deserted changing area, by people who had never returned from the sea, like the ones they had erected the memorial to in front of the lighthouse at the other end of the promenade. People are really swimming, I thought and was delighted by the chance of seeing somebody dive into the cold, rolling Atlantic Ocean, although at the thought of swimming I felt a chill, in spite of the sun, which was glowing like a white spot on a blue eye. I sat down on the wet, black rocks beneath the pier and watched a sparse procession of bathers, both male and female, all older townspeople who had probably been bathing here since childhood; they walked in silence, backs straight, with the practised poise of swimmers, the men in simple blue linen knee-length trunks, the women in black one-piece swimsuits, everyone with close-fitting rubber caps on their heads; they walked one after the other, and, in fact, you could sense a certain restraint in their step, as if by the strength of their will and thought they had slowed down gravity, which became weaker with every movement of their body as they approached the edge of the pier; by now they should be able to run or dive far beyond the world's horizon, but the old, veteran swimmers suddenly slowed their step, not because they feared the cold sea but because, I thought when I was still seeing them in my mind, there was in their attitude towards the sea, and towards the world, something ritualistic, ceremonial, aristocratic and free, all at the same time, something that had surely been inscribed in the bone and muscle, in the soul, of these early-spring swimmers even before they had ever jumped into the sea, so that now, as I lay on a rock beneath the pier and observed them, the bathers walked along the concrete platform as on a promenade intended for no one else and nothing else but exercise, of the body and of the spirit, and delight in the sea; that is how I still see them today in my mind, just as I did then, when I was first watching them, as they walked to the rusty iron ladders that dropped sharply into the rolling sea. A moment later, without hesitating or gasping at the touch of the icy sea rushing at their unprotected bodies, each of them, one after the other, descended bravely into the dark waves. Soon they were swimming; I saw only their caps, rising above and dipping below the surface. They didn't swim far, just a few strong, slow strokes, turned, floated for a moment on their backs with their arms spread wide, dead men and women, and then with the same indomitable poise climbed up the ladder out of the sea and into the cold wind. They undressed in the changing area without shame or vocal comment, put on their city clothes and with their hair still wet left the swimming pier and returned to their everyday chores, just as they had probably been doing for years, for decades. The sun again hid quickly behind the clouds, the dark shadows of the sky were swimming among the waves, which rushed relentlessly across the pier, and instantly the tower with the diving platforms, which nobody had dived from today, lost its summer magic, its holiday languor and reverie, and in their place a smell of dereliction rose to the surface, of rancid

seaweed lying in heaps on the sand, all of which enveloped this day – for me a day of celebration, which I had decided to spend quietly – in a very different atmosphere, I thought as I stood up, muddy and chilled from the sea sand and from the sea, which was spraying across the pier, and it had started raining, too, even before the last bathers had disappeared; today I am forty-five years old, I thought, and will have something to remember the day by. I saw a large tanker immersed in the choppy sea moving slowly out of the bay; by evening it would be far out in the open sea in the middle of the bottomless plain, far from the last lighthouse of home, but this ship would certainly return one day, I was sure of it. The red Toyota in which Gjini drove me to Clifden (when I first saw the diving tower), where I was going for a few days to finish my manuscript in peace, was constantly losing its way on the narrow, winding road that rose and fell, flanked by low stone walls, through the bleak, scorched and empty Connemara landscape. The grass was low and flattened, yellowish; the trees, the once-abundant green woods that had covered a large part of the island, had been cut down by the English over their centuries-long occupation, Gjini said, and the few houses along the empty road, all low and white, which are scattered through this windy land, appeared to be abandoned, the windows bolted shut with heavy blue, green or red wooden frames; beyond the stone walls that stretched far and wide across the land, for kilometres and miles, from the sea and far away over the bare hills blanketed by white clouds, thick and motionless, there was nothing but silent nature; there's nothing here, Gjini said, when we stopped at a crossroads of wholly identical roads; narrow signs with arrows marking routes in all directions; whichever way we turned we would come to Clifden, but which of these completely identical roads should we choose? We could go by a twisting, narrow road that weaved its way slowly right by the sea; nobody can measure the length of that road, Gjini said, cursing; or we had the option of taking a bad, half-deserted road through a stony landscape – like driving on the moon, Gjini said, again with a curse; he preferred to find a more modern, wider and, especially, faster road, since we're running late, he said, initially in the stiff acquired English he had learned upon arrival in his new country, and then, after irritably answering a few phone calls – my wife, is all he said – he started swearing in a stiff, brusque, monosyllabic Albanian. I came to Galway eleven years ago, and when I moved here I didn't speak a word of English; everything I know I learned here and everything I have I made here; this is a strange, beautiful and in many ways cursed country, Gjini said and suddenly turned right, as if finally deciding, although he was not at all sure it was the right road. I'm in a hurry, he said; I have an important meeting at three and can't be late; my future is being decided today, you understand, he said; my life is being decided today, he said and looked me in the eye. For a second the red Toyota was racing along on its own, out of control, between the black walls, bouncing over deep holes gouged out of the rough asphalt by wind and incessant rain, which now still lay hidden somewhere in the motionless clouds that watched us, or maybe not, from the tops of the bleak, dark hills. You can't predict the weather here; it's always the same: unforeseeable, changeable, and in its own way monotonous – no snow, no hot sun. That's why people here sit for days and nights in dark, dirty pubs, Gjini, my driver and occasional guide, concluded. I smiled; you'll see soon enough, he said imploringly, I know, I've been here eleven years; I work fifteen, sixteen hours a day to feed myself and my family, while people here think only about whiskey and beer; you can't make arrangements with anybody, they don't know what clocks are for, just like they can't predict the weather; they keep you waiting for hours and hours, like the sun that comes out every once in a while, but in between it's always raining; for foreigners, this is a cursed country. Sourly, somewhat guardedly, and not too convincingly, I smiled; I didn't believe him; I didn't want to believe any of it, how could I? This was my first time here, my first bright day, even if the forecast was ominous, and he was an immigrant, a foreigner from a land I knew only by hearsay and about which I knew just three words: Skenderbeg, a folk hero, a half-mythological figure whose name I was able to pronounce mainly because of a heavy, horrible brandy I

once tried, which was my only real physical contact with this small, mysterious Balkan land, and to judge solely on the basis of that, the people here would no doubt like it, based, of course, on what Gjini had said about them; I also knew a few bizarre details about the former dictator Enver Hoxha, mainly relating to his unimaginable cruelty, about which, I thought, Gjini would certainly have a great deal more to say later; and, of course, I knew the only bright name from his godforsaken land, a name that was personally dear to me because it was so closely tied to my work and, in a way, to the reason I now found myself here, in the middle of this seemingly desolate landscape with the threat of a near-deluge hanging over me, when decisions would soon be made about the life and death of an Albanian immigrant, which is to say, about the fate of all of us who at that moment were in unknown lands, in places without name or memory, and were left merely to silent supplications, to the mercy of the sky and the weather, to eternally repeating the names of our nearest, our dearest, our beloved children and wives – so then, that single bright name, a name that would allow me to make an impression on Gjini without coming off as a fool or a fraud, was the name Kadare, the writer. Yes, he said, Kadare is great, and it sounded like truth, for him, for me and for the entire unpeopled landscape around us. It was as if he was telling the dry grass, the black stones and the cloudy weather that he and I were protected by this name. Then, for just a moment, the rain came down, a brief shower; the road broadened as soon as the sun came out; on the asphalt, big white clouds were shining; they floated across the crystal blue on which we were driving; the stone walls spread apart and ran off beneath a hill, where the fog was being slowly torn into big white sheets of blank paper, as if reminding me not to forget why I had journeyed so far. Look, my driver said, who the past few miles had been going faster and faster, but now he had suddenly slowed the car and was looking to the right, in the direction of a valley that curved away, far from the main road; over there, next to the old road to Clifden, standing by a lake, is Kylemore Abbey – which I could also read on a road sign; yes, I said; the name continued to echo in my ears for some time, it was somehow familiar and comforting to me, yet magnificently foreign; I've been there several times – it's a wonderful manor, Gjini said knowledgeably; when I was a student at the University of Galway – it was only my third year but already I could write fluent English, Gjini stated proudly – I wrote a research paper about it, right here, in these desolate mountains and damp marshy valleys, which can also have their beauty; in those days I would explore them up and down, comb them, you might say, on my long morning walks when those pampered Irish students, without any real under-standing or joy, were still asleep, since even then I noticed that they were mainly interested in the out-of-the-way pubs, although, in fact, there was only one pub here at the time and it was nearly an hour's walk from the manor, thank god, so they could only escape to it in the evening, Gjini said and smiled a little shyly; well, we spent a few days there and did intensive research on that imposing manor and its sur-roundings. You seem to know everything, I thought, when Gjini said

that on his arrival in Galway, when he didn't know a single word of the language (he said again), he did whatever came along at first; he sold sandwiches at the bus station, around the corner from the hotel where he had picked me up that morning, and cleaned offices at night and similar things until he learned enough English to pass the language test; then he enrolled as a regular student in Irish cultural heritage studies, which was something between history, archaeology and ethnology, he added, trying to give me a clearer idea. That's why I was chosen to drive you and be your guide, he said. Kylemore Abbey, he said, as if he was spelling it out by syllable, was doing a crossword and wanted to be sure the letters fitted the squares, or maybe he had just now discovered in the sound of the name, which he naturally pronounced with a slight accent, something that for many people here would for ever remain hidden; Kylemore Abbey, I now repeated the name to myself so I wouldn't forget it, although I was sure I had already heard about this place, somewhere beside a dark lake, hidden beneath the mountains, as I made a quick mental picture of it, an imaginary sketch – a method used by writers that's not unlike what painters do, and maybe I learned it from them – I normally use a sketch when I compose my texts; this is the only reason I'm on this road right now, I thought, and I need peace to do it; I'm at rest, neither asleep nor awake, when I assemble my compositions out of sentences; I move words around and invert them, try to estimate the length of the text, and somewhere, deep in the background, the text takes on different colours for me; the black lines are usually long and dense; next come planes of pure white, which are nevertheless full of meaning, weight- less meaning; the chapters blend together, from brown, grey and green to shades of dark red, the higher the point from which I observe the emerging inner landscape, which I still read as a text that in that fleet- ing moment, more tenuous than the named moment when I write this line, is being born somewhere deep, washing in like distant waves that will maybe never reach my eyes; it is carried by nameless clouds, shadows with first names and last names but bodiless, and then all of it slowly, as in silent reverie, transforms into sculptural reliefs,

landscape paintings, portraits, into the earth, the ceaseless expansion of the universe, and at some later time, when they have long withdrawn themselves from the visible world, I again summon them from memory, and only then am I able to capture something of the beauty I was allowed to see in my time, to capture it in letters, words, sentences, chapters, to hold these in space, just as something summoned me from memory and held me in this life – this was running through my mind when the landscape in front of us suddenly opened into a wide, bright valley bordered by soft carpets of golden grass and encircled by bare rocky mountain crests, above which shone, at last, a transparent, clear and endless blue. Next to the road, which led through a place that was neither a town nor a village, a dark stone church was the only thing that jutted prominently into the sunny early afternoon; on the other side of the road I saw an empty petrol station with the word 'Topaz' written in large boastful letters, but then the road took a sharp rise and I could see nothing more over the hill; Eldorado might be hiding there, I thought, but I'll never be able to discover it; throughout eternity nothing will speak of it, testify to it, except Poe's poem. Accelerating, as if we were crossing the finish line at the end of a long car race, Gjini pulled off the main road into a large asphalt courtyard. We stopped next to a long low building with a long raised concrete platform in front; a big sign with the name of the place, Clifden, hung on the wall; the façade was clad in freshly painted wooden boards; beneath the tin awning that covered half the platform, somebody had carefully arranged a few new café tables, which stood lonely in the white sun that had appeared soon after the storm; it was like I had arrived at a remote country train station where no train had stopped in ages, but there were no tracks anywhere, no clouds of steam from overheated locomotives, no train whistles and, most of all, no passengers with bags, sitting or walking expectantly up and down the platform; there was nobody anywhere to be seen; I was the last to arrive; I had the feeling that there was nothing left here but ghosts and stories, hidden, wrapped in the silence of the houses, buried in the graves, lurking trapped in books, washed away by floods, swallowed by mighty nature, which was slowly and inexorably taking everything culture had ever made, but I hoped I was wrong; although I had come here to find peace for my work, I had no desire to be the last and only passenger still waiting for a train that would never take him away.

The water left on the tables by the recent storm was dripping slowly on to the ground, tiny tears glistening like scattered marbles that fell from a child's playful hands and rolled away, off the platform and on to the train tracks; when I later recalled them, I think they brought an unexpected warm smile to my face, which still carries me today; at the time, however, I was standing with my bag in my hands in the middle of the empty courtyard, not really knowing which way or where to go; Gjini had long ago raced off to his meeting, maybe taking the same last train I had just left, and the red Toyota was twisting and turning between the stone walls; maybe it is twisting and turning even now as I write these lines; a man, an Albanian immigrant, will for ever be hurrying like Sisyphus to a business meeting in the city where decisions will be made about his life or death, as he had said earlier; I was sure that this time he would certainly be late, since he couldn't get back to the city in an hour – or maybe he would arrive on time, since you can't rely on anybody here, they keep you waiting for hours, even if it's a matter of life or death, Gjini had said. It was already late afternoon; long thick shadows were almost completely covering the courtyard; the only thing still sunlit was the raised platform, which had, in fact, once served as the railway platform; this I soon learned, when, with my big suitcase on wheels and my other bags hanging from my shoulders, I announced myself at the reception desk. Behind the long counter, in semi-darkness, sat the receptionist, absorbed in her work as she rummaged through piles of papers. Clearly, I was one of only a few guests, maybe the only guest to arrive at this hour, on this day, in this week; there was nobody anywhere except the two of us, each absorbed in our own thoughts. The many low tables and deep armchairs and two-seat sofas, all neatly arranged from the counter to the large windows with their diaphanous white curtains, which fell to the floor in regular, well-spaced folds, like sea waves when the tide comes in, reminded me of many paintings I had seen here; everything was still and silent, although I had the feeling that somewhere in the background, from a different room, there was a voice, the hum of a radio, turned down but never turned off, neither by the day shift nor the night shift. This radio hum, something between

speech, music and chaos, remains with me even now, as I write these lines, and I believe I will even hear it when I sit in silence after completing my work, maybe then most of all, as if it had gained strength in my memory, and again I will see the light caught in the folds, in the pleats of the curtains, which were becoming darker, nearly grey, like the sea beneath storm clouds. Suddenly I was touched by a thought, soft and translucent, like the shadow of a bird in flight, the thought that this playful tickling of sunlight had touched my cheek before; I closed my eyes and ducked beneath the hem of the embroidered white blanket in my high blue carriage, its canopy trimmed in a dangling fringe in which the afternoon light had interlaced itself, rocking me to sleep as the carriage rumbled slowly through town along a dusty road; now I hear again a murmur from somewhere far off, as if from a different world, which I can't see from my golden ship; is it laughter, an invitation? Is it merely a dream or my earliest longing for truth? I can't be sure, but maybe that tiny head hidden safe in clean cotton and fine feathers fragrant with Mama, who smoothly, melodically and proudly pushed the blue baby carriage up to the big window, a window larger than the azure sky with big drowsy sheep floating across it, but now the view of the sky was veiled by a light diaphanous curtain, unpatterned, exactly like the one in this lonely hotel, I thought, a curtain that each of us must one day open for ourselves, like love, and conquer the fear of death that lies behind every window, every lonely tree, and also behind all the suns in what perhaps is the most beautiful, the only, universe – at that moment, then, my tiny head with its healthy, plump red cheeks was sinking into soft sleep, or maybe this was the day that that head first woke from sleep, wrenching itself away from something big, mysterious and beautiful, something I would be searching for my entire life and which I also search for now, as I write these lines.

I opened the map on my tablet and surveyed the lonely landscape that went sharply down towards the sea next to the road in front of me, as I now saw on the map; while I waited for the satellites to find me and determine my position, I once more travelled slowly with my eye through the inscribed knot of roads along the marked bike route; this is where I am, I thought, as I slid my thumb and forefinger lightly over the screen and enlarged the map so I could read the names of the few local streets I'd left behind, and found my road; here I've just gone past the point where it splits into two narrow lanes, I determined – although I was thinking about which way to go, which lane to choose, when, a few minutes before, I stopped for a moment in front of a tall, blackened, stone Celtic cross with a dark aureole that stood on the road out of Clifden, and all at once it dawned on me that the solid stone circles on old Celtic crosses could be depictions of the solar corona, like the signature or mark of the ancient, sunny island soul that centuries ago inscribed and enrolled itself in early Christian tradition, certainly long before the ancient Slavic tribes arrived and settled permanently in my own country, between Pannonia and the Adriatic. Here and on the nearby Aran Islands, which Gjini and I would visit a few days later – on these wild, remote Irish shores, which right up until Columbus's daring transoceanic expeditions were thought to be

the absolute end of the known and familiar civilized world, a conviction long shared by famous philosophers, inspired poets and enraptured stargazers, but their lofty thoughts and profound outpourings were, with the sad collapse of the empire, increasingly marginal; with the fall of the old regime and overshadowed by the rise of something new, which was proclaiming faith, hope and love, antiquity lost its sparkle and shine, Gjini said later, as we waited one rainy morning for the hydrofoil that would take us to the last island of our world, which lay far out of sight, submerged in churning waves and veiled by a thick, heavy curtain of rain. That's why the arrival and settlement of a handful of black-robed monks in this desolate landscape meant the end, a full stop in the great chapter, in the book that would still have to be written, Gjini said after an interval, when he returned with the big white tickets for the ferry, speaking softly, discreetly, but too obviously for him to cover up his constantly smouldering but falsely concealed rage, his indignation, at the weather but mostly at the fate that had brought him here, to wind and rain, to live among people whose nature he would never understand – not now, as we kept checking the dark-grey sky between the black eaves and lifeless façades of houses with curtained windows streaming with the early morning rain that poured down, pounded, from every direction, water coursing down the roads, spilling off the pavements, gushing from the gutters, clattering over tin roofs, and my Albanian guide could not make peace with himself or with a world that, before our eyes, was enacting the Biblical legend of the universal flood; nor later, when we were all sitting, soaked to the skin but seemingly rescued, on the narrow benches of a ramshackle bus – the journey, after all, had just begun and the promised land was still far away. Pressing my head against the window, I gazed out at the dark and drowning town; I couldn't speak, words were like rain, they fell into the sea, into the formless waters, deep and horizonless, just as it was described in the first pages of the Bible I had found the night before in a drawer in the hotel room. So the word, the story, really was in the beginning; a hundred thousand years before the Creation a poem was echoing in the void, I thought; the end of the world and its silence will soon be here, and we, soaking wet tourists on the first morning bus, an immigrant and two writers far from home, far from our languages, are rushing to catch the last ark, as the animals chosen by Captain Noah had once done; not to worry, Gjini said, we already have our tickets for the ferry. I couldn't move; soaked, sleepy, with a veil of anxiety in my heart, for a long time I just watched the torrential streams, the cheerless pastures bordered by stone walls, the abandoned houses next to them, everything slowly being carried off by water; all I remember are soaking wet figures stamping their feet in the mud; they had spread newspapers over their heads and were trying in vain to light their cigarettes, but soon, even before the little flame was glowing for a brief second between their huddled heads, nature had already washed out the bold print, the morning headlines, and devoured the flimsy paper, which was swimming with the current towards the blocked sewer drain. In the beginning was the word, I remembered reading during the night, but that was yesterday; now it was the second day and the fog was still floating above the waters. So, just like us a little while before, as we waited soaking wet for the early bus to the harbour, monks had come here a thousand years ago, in rain and thick fog, in the name of faith, hope and love, as they said, carrying not only the Holy Gospels in their packs but all the knowledge and all the great mysteries of Greece and Rome, and so rescued them from fire, sword and oblivion. As you can see, Gjini said, these fervent men devoted to prayer and learning bequeathed to this lost nation, along with the precious books they translated from Arabic and the ancient languages, also a marvellous monastic and early Christian architecture, and especially, and not least of all, he underscored with a little smile, the recipe for that miracle potion we call beer, which is what the local poor, who even today can flare up at a moment's notice, most quickly and easily mastered. It was maybe in the late sixth or seventh century that these inspired men set off across the devastated continent in search of a place far from swords, far from crosses, where they could write in peace and quiet and concentration – not too long, in any case, after Ancient Rome collapsed in dust and on its ruins, in its ashes and

blood, you might say, the legend of the murdered Son blossomed forth and spread across the earth like dawn over the sea, especially the mysterious tale of infinite and never-understood, always-resurrected love, which conquers death and darkness and so is the only true Sun on the cross, which each of us carries in the dark interior of our heart as memory and inspiration, as was told to us and passed on to us in Scripture, amen.

By the old roadside cross where the two lanes split, as if facing temptation, I had stopped and got off the bicycle, and with the tablet on my knees was waiting for the satellites to find me, for only thus would I exist again, have my inner landscape returned to me, be re-inscribed on the refreshed map of names, although invisible, although merely virtual, like a memory from which a future text was only now emerging, with the shape and atmosphere of something past but never lost, as if illuminated by sunbeams breaking through floating clouds – so then, I was pondering and weighing the situation, although everything had been decided long before, even before I got here, maybe even before I was born. An arrow on a roadside sign, a marker beneath the cross, pointed to the right, at a road that gradually climbed away from the sea and curved along a ridge or the edge of an overhang until it reached the furthest point on the coast, a low green spit that penetrated deep into the sea; inscribed there was the name of the last place on this earth: Kingstown. On the tablet, the terrain appeared inhospitable, even at a glance – stony and harsh, like the refracted glare of a landscape in the eyes, with the same dull parchment-yellow colouring you see in chronic liver patients; there in the distance, in the City of Our Lord, the King's Town, where the last and only human trail was leading, the road – I was still following it on the electronic map – turned away from the sea and ran along the other side of the ridge, right beside the shore, where the sea again cut deep into the interior of the island, back to the point where I then was resting, and so traced the longer strand of the road junction, nearly thirteen miles long, which had been christened the Sky Road – from the name alone I guessed that at a certain point the designated route must ascend high above the coast, towards the sky, so it will be an arduous bike ride uphill, I thought, but the journey must also be scenic, photogenic, with high cliffs, I imagined, that drop into the Atlantic and only a few sparse hamlets, scattered houses standing alone in clearings, which I now could see alongside stone ruins, amid villages abandoned long ago – or maybe only recently – and huddled beneath the dark-green shadows of the island's hills. A dark-grey hand-chiselled stone, painstakingly mortared into the body of an abandoned house, with its notion of the eternal family defying loneliness, the rain and longing for home, far from any eyes; maybe, I thought, the message of birth or death might have been delivered, from the threshold of one deserted house to the door of the next, by mad wailing into the deaf and foggy night, if only the eternal wind here didn't howl like wandering ghosts from the empty houses, ghosts who travel past on the great Gulf Stream, if only it didn't swallow up every human word, whether kind or cruel, I later thought when I was telling Gjini about the road. Possibly, the souls are returning on the Gulf Stream, drowned, perished, banished in the years of the Great Famine, or maybe all these scattered

lost souls are now, in fact, arriving from America and Canada, where their forgotten relatives had sailed on empty stomachs in ramshackle arks with potato knives and pallid hopes in their pockets, and the tiny beam from Mutton Light, shining through the rain, the fog and the waves, was their last and only desire, which travels through generations, from mothers and fathers, from grandfathers and great-grandfathers, and is passed on, hidden in the language, to those not yet born, like an eternal dream that comes to us on the invisible stream of consciousness, that whispers to us like memory, before it is drowned, before it shatters on the shores of our former home. It lies in a landscape eternally green; it shines in the fog after the rain that floats among the ruins, somewhere in a faraway fairy-tale land. The other, shorter strand of the junction where I had stopped to get my bearings went left from the old cross, along Beach Road, as it said on my tablet, down to the sea, which was still out of view; of course, I had been wondering for just a moment which road to take when the satellites searching for me from the edge of space found me. A tiny dot had been flashing and circling slowly over a virtual point beside the road on the Google map until the satellites intercepted and correlated my precise position in the imaginary landscape; then the dot stopped moving, coming to rest on the road precisely where I was standing; that's me, I thought, and as I

slid my thumb and forefinger across the tablet to shrink the map, I saw my pulsating point, the beating of a heart, melt into an ever vaster landscape, as if my eye had separated from my body and was ascending high into the sky, swiftly, to the edge of space, from where I could see the entire planet. Among the billions of similar virtual hearts pulsating, trembling in fear, yearning and bleeding, the only one I saw on the electronic map was my own other body, a digital, silently pulsating marker in a grid of parallels and meridians, which might stay there for ever if at that moment the tablet slipped out of my hands and I didn't pick it up again, or if I simply buried it there, beneath the old Celtic cross, and for at least a while divorced myself from my virtual body, which goes with me always and everywhere like the shadow that once followed the lonely pilgrim. I was instantly in a fairy-tale; I remembered Oscar Wilde's story 'The Fisherman and His Soul', in which the Irishman placed a great temptation in front of his enamoured fisherman: if the mortal fisherman wished to marry the beautiful mermaid he had fallen immortally in love with, he would first have to give up his soul. Despite the arguments and entreaties of his beautiful soul, the lover was prepared to do anything to fulfil his vow of love. He begged help from the witches, who gave him a little knife, with which at sunset, without a second thought, standing on the shore, maybe not far from where I was standing at that moment, he cut off his shadow, which was the body of his soul. Who is the traveller, the body or its shadow, us or that point on the map? Gjini and I wondered later; here everything is still like a fairy-tale – you'll see soon enough, Gjini said after a pause, I'll never be able to understand it. I took a few panoramic photos with my phone; I rotated slowly, holding the camera above the horizon in my raised right hand, the way landscape painters used to do with brush and sketchbook, from left to right – to remember, I thought, like the sun, which remembers its path; then I simply got on my bike, turned off the tablet and telephone, and tore off downhill to the seashore, on a road that ended by a boathouse. It wasn't far – a narrow, cracked road, bordered by a low stone wall overgrown with flowering shrubbery and dry thorn bushes, which had woven themselves into the rusty barbed wire that kept sheep and horses from being lost for ever in the island's trackless wilds, as I could merely assume, since on my descent to the sea, which I soon caught sight of in the bay far below, I neither saw nor heard a single animal – only the barbed wire remains in my memory. The shadow of a cloud was floating over the bay, like a soft flying carpet trimmed with golden ribbons of light, which were dancing in the bay after the storm. I took a few more photos of the shore, the boathouse in the distance, a self-portrait, and a panoramic shot of the sky, and afterwards ran through the low, meticulously mowed grass towards the bicycle, which stood alone beside a concrete wall. As for me, I was still all over the place; I had the feeling I had gone too far, that I was approaching that invisible boundary from where it's a long way to everywhere, my trail was getting lost, more and more footprints were missing, were being erased by the wind, sinking like the white furrows behind a ship; it occurred to me that I was far from home and only the satellites high above the clouds knew where I was, knew who I was, and that there were more and more of us, lost and lonely, travelling too far; every second somebody flees, travels, crawls on their hands and feet, dreams about a journey, yearns for the unattainable, aeroplanes take off and land, cars circle like predatory birds on city

arteries and slowly vanish into one-way streets; silently or with the hum of a radio inside us we move through other worlds, parallel and temporary, made of photographic memories and drawn only on online maps. The thought of electronic blackout, wire-free silence, deletion from databases and address books, is still far away, an unbelieved threat that smoulders like a dark dawn, radiates from the cosmic background; the curving, relativistic gleam of hope for deliverance is stronger and deeper, persistently illuminating us like an innate idea of infinity; we are comforted by the eternal pulsation of the cursor on our black, wide, flat monitors, with profiles open day and night, with comments, and especially with billions of our favourite photographs on remote, invisible servers, along with the dates of personal holidays, home videos, browsed books and desired locations. It will all perhaps outlive us, be saved in an archive, in an intact, compressed record, our stories will long be traceable, readable, visible, even after the death of the temporary human vehicle, and will maybe, right up to the universal cooling, be copied over and over, pasted and inscribed on the cosmic consciousness, as Gregor Strniša, our poet of dark stars, once wrote, or maybe it's true that, insecure and shallow, we merely post our photographs and comments on Facebook hopelessly, with trembling hands.

Like a mirage at the end of the road, without reflection or gleam, dark and grey, a geometric plane shadowed in pencil on a yellowed sheet of drawing paper – that's what the sea looked like – shallow, motionless, monastery beer spilled into eternity on to a black stone floor, but mainly trapped in a wide, ever wider, nearly limitless landscape; the nearer I was to the shore, the greater, the more impressive was the bay, in the middle of which stood a black lighthouse on sharp rocks, no bigger than a wizard's ring, hovering on the motionless surface, while the master's pale hand, still wearing it proudly, had long ago sunk beneath the sea. Without braking, I went down off the asphalt road on to a wide, neatly mowed grassy area in front of the boathouse and rode up to the sea. I leaned the bicycle against a low breakwater that was protecting the lawn from the high tide and slowly made my way over the grey sand, between the slippery rocks, the black pebbles and the rotting seaweed, into the oneness, the residue and abandonment, the world that remained when that sunken, dead arm last unclenched its hand and released the silt on which I now stepped, I thought as the smell washed over me, as if I was standing in an old, abandoned, invisible maritime cemetery, eerily beautiful none the less, like the romantic landscapes of the Old Masters. Death comes here to rest, the thought ran through me, after guiding the wandering, lost souls every day on their final journey, taking them far across the sea, to invisible islands chiselled from soft white light and overgrown with tall, dark silences, like a lyric nocturne in the middle of the sea; and after traversing the width and breadth of Europe, this is where she lays down her cold, sharp work tool, on this remote and hidden shore, and maybe for the first time in her eternal deathly life she lets slip from her shoulders the foggy shroud that shields her dark and hollow radiance, which pulses like a lighthouse from another world. Now I was hearing death with every cautious step I took in the black sand, sensing it in the swell, the gleam of the motionless waters, in every story, every marker along the road; I saw it on the threshold of every lonely deserted house standing open to the sky, roofless, without window or door, without a crucifix or the Book, which the fugitives

had taken with them, in good faith perhaps or in mortal terror, on their uncertain voyage across the sea that lay in front of me, and which, if not for ever lost or at the bottom of the sea, are now holy relics safely stored again in a drawer, in a new home across the Atlantic, as a memory of forebears, of a lineage with a forgotten name, and with a consciousness of ancestry, the dark trace of identity that still rings in the soul like a terrible wind in a dream; standing by the shore, I heard it, I saw it everywhere then – death, resting here. The scene, a stirring ritual of farewell, which apart from love is the single most deeply binding gesture that lies in a person's heart (as the poet Boris A. Novak described it), was repeated, was literally doubled, as if I was hearing the echo of my inner voice, the first time I stood in front of the painting *An Island Funeral*, then on display at the Galway City Museum, which I visited one afternoon after my return to the city – but first I went with Gjini to the place he had told me about on the drive to Clifden, when we had first met.

A long, narrow road through a gorge, next to the dark, still shores of lakes encircled by mountain peaks, which I couldn't distinguish from the great veiled white clouds, grey on the edges, that were gathering and rolling through the damp green vapours of the morning air and without accent or nuance in their description settling on

the muted orange wasteland, the damp and stifling, heavy, crumbling earth, which was hardly breathing, was gasping like tired, smoke-filled lungs, all this dripping damp and piles of mouldering, scorched grass lying on the earth were like a moist fuel, a black fire, burning earth – peat they call it here – which once warmed the walls of houses now a century deserted, which are scattered like lonely lost lambs across the entire country, bleating their harsh and gloomy, mysterious and mournful, but also beautiful and inaccessible, even cruel, Irish poem for human destiny, in an elusive tonality between the pathos of Gothic narrative and elemental folk balladry, or, maybe better, in the style of the romantic landscape painting that I was only now discovering here. That's how I remember my first trip with the study group to this gloomy, hidden landscape, godforsaken you might say, which is how it seemed to me at the time. I remember that we stopped a few times on the way for no good reason, which from my student experience in my old homeland I found almost unthinkable; I mean that students would simply go trotting off when they had obligations or, worse, would forge friendships, be both drinking partners and academic colleagues, with the professors, Gjini said; so, as I said, whenever the sun came out for a moment and lit up the black surface of the lakes and the murmur of the mountain streams, we would run off far from the cars, away from the road, deep into the peatlands, hiding from the wind and the damp morning fog, which rolled down from the bare reddish peaks that wouldn't be green for a while still, since winter had not yet breathed its last, and we would lie down between the tall, evenly cut, carefully stacked piles of black, decomposing earth, the peat, which was drying in the meagre sun. There, sheltered by earth, as if we were just now being born, we smoked cigarettes and drained bottles of black beer, and then moved on, a ragtag band of scholars, a brotherhood of professors and students. Although I was a foreigner, an immigrant, and still learning the jargon of high academia, and was moreover the oldest student in the group, a person who with some effort and for his own survival was merely skilfully concealing his homesickness, swallowing his anger, the disappointment and despair of the refugee, which were still mixed with will, with determination for a new beginning, and with inconsolable nostalgia, which, in fact, appeared and found its true name only later, when I had somehow got on my feet, as soon as I sensed that we would somehow make it, would be able to transplant ourselves, put down at least shallow roots in the new soil, and even later, when I would come back again and stop here, mostly on my own but occasionally with my family, and take long walks, when my second education, if you will, was successfully behind me (my first degree I had received long before in Tirana, in political science and journalism) – that's when I realized we were in some way alike, we can't hide or suppress our background, no matter where we are from or where we are born, we're made out of a substance, like soil or an island, and on top of it, nostalgia, Gjini said, and the Irish understand this. I still grab every available moment I can to get in the car and escape here, to this magical, deserted, dark and inhospitable landscape, and for at least an hour or so I put on the mud boots I keep in the car and go for a walk over the damp ground, even when rain is pouring down on me or fog is hiding me; under its protection, in its sheer, shimmering whiteness, as if I was floating high above the waters, in the rediscovered memory of the landscape of my childhood, when I was similarly always getting lost in hollows and pastures, where no foreign word could reach me – my only world, our only world, was built solely of names, with no questions asked about meaning or significance – there, under the protection of silence and always the same faces, which accompanied me from my birth to my emigration and will in a sense be with me until I die, which I feel more and more each year, there I remembered and named things with a mere glance, I lived in an endless, silent and humble presence, there was nothing I missed or needed, and my whole reality, even the imagination in which I lived my childhood freedom, is still somewhere deep inside me, and from it, from this eternal source, I learn again every day unknown words, search for the deeper, the deceitful meaning of my second life, my immigrant life, Gjini said and was silent for a moment, as if he'd forgotten his point, or maybe we had missed a turn again, I thought. I didn't see any sign or road marker, I said tentatively, and, in the awkwardness of the moment and just enough to let me wade through the silence, I started assiduously wiping the misted windscreen with my sleeve. When you are far from your language, you are also far from your home, more and more each day, and the distance increases and deepens with every new word; the lost word is usurped, seemingly replaced, by the other, more convincing, better word, which everyone can understand but which is still foreign; the immigrant, this eternal guardian but also suppresser of his own language, knows that the loss, the void, the dissolved malt of forgetting within it, which he tenaciously envelops and fills with learning, which is the only vaccine against loneliness, despair and madness, is nevertheless irreplaceable, painful and incurable, like love, Gjini said and noticeably slowed the speed at which we were driving. That's why I come here, he said and looked off into the distance, to relearn the only language left from my childhood, the language of silence, of looking. I walk in silence and observe the landscape, the earth, I lose myself in the fog and soon I can't make out anything any more; I don't know who I am or even where I come from, I don't even remember what language I'm thinking in, what language I name the world in. Then I write a poem. Totally wet, totally sweaty or totally cold, I drag myself back to the car and take a notebook out of the glove compartment, one that Jane gave me, and for a few minutes or until it gets dark, which is when, no matter what, I go home for supper since my family always expects me on the dot, so before I go home, I write. And I always try to translate every word, from one language to the other, so the poem from which I am made doesn't burn up like earth, like black fire, peat, as they say here. At home, of course, we all speak Albanian around the table, not just my wife and older boy, but even our little girl, who was born here. Enough so she doesn't forget where we come from, Gjini said and, taking a long bend in the road, he silently and with unusual concentration slowed the car, as if he was getting ready to make an important announcement; I could feel the tension and weight of his silence; then came a rumbling sound and a moment later the grey and weary road was flooded, the surface heaving with water; the storm, which came down into the gorge like an avalanche from the surrounding peaks, poured on to the road and the car was carried as if in the middle of a turbulent ocean. All I could see through the misted windscreen, which I was now wiping frantically with my sweater sleeve, were long translucent ribbons of water pouring down faster and faster, harder and harder from the low clouds, like a densely woven curtain; despite the gusting wind, which was constantly shifting the direction of the waves on the road, the heavy drops were falling to the earth in perfectly parallel lines, as in some ideal garden of pure Euclidean forms, and the very next moment, even before we had completed the bend in the road, even before I had made another desperate sweep of my arm to open a tiny slit for my eye, which searched for a view of the sky, as if seeking an answer or making a request – that's when Gjini, with a curse on his lips and a curse in the corner of his eye, slammed on the brakes. There was pounding and popping, like stones hailing down on us, and when the roar of the rushing waters beneath the wheels had subsided a little, all we could do was gather our strength. Gjini, without a word of warning or any indication, hastily shoved open the door and I saw not a river but a turbulent sea racing past, and then this man, my guide, the only creature I knew in

the middle of this deluge, stepped knee-high into the raging waters, in his shirtsleeves, with just a linen hat on his head, and vanished in the diagonal rain. His blurry shadow, which I tried to catch through the mist on the foggy windscreen, evaporated like a soul cut from its body, even before I could wipe the glass with my hand.

I remember the light, a diffuse, radiant, literally white light, that flickered in the clouds on the horizon as I made my way with solemn step slowly back to the city, thinking that I would have something lovely to remember the day by, for this is a day I experience as a personal holiday; the diving tower, where I had spent the morning, was now far away, at the other end of the coastal road, and here, in the bay in front of the city, the sea was surrounding Mutton Light, the lighthouse, which was no less immersed in this unearthly noonday light; the sea, then, was bringing to the city the light, which broke into pieces, glinted along the coast, and lifted itself above the city on a mighty wind, settled among the hidden streets and smuggled itself into the language, hid itself deep in the speech – I heard its hum, its loud laughter, waves breaking against the rocks in the local harbour, I heard them, waves and wind, echoing in the voices of the group at the bar, who too early in the day were cooling their hot hands on glasses of black beer in a dark pub; maybe they were hiding in here, I thought, to give their eyes a rest from the dazzling light that was shining outside like ultimate truth; who knows who the drinkers of this late morning will still remember, who they will call to mind, even wake from the dead, now and for evermore, with glasses of dark beer in their hands in a gloomy backstreet pub, hiding in an extinguished lighthouse tower, in their minds by now somewhere far outside, just a bit more and they'll sail away again for a moment, bid farewell to the city and the last lighthouse, drown in language, in incomprehensible laughter, which shines from their wild, wounded, glistening and most sorrowful eyes, like the surface of the light that accompanied me that morning on the narrow path, which was none the less full of joggers and

dog-walkers, along the coast from Gratton House to the museum. And soon I was sailing with them, with everyone who had once fled hunger, departing these shores to somewhere far across the ocean – they took me on board, these too-early drinkers, who now stood on the street in front of the pub smoking, as if on the deck of a ship that had been lost long ago; from time to time they would check the narrow strip of sky above the crowded rooftops and then hide their heads again between their shoulders; they were like seabirds, only filled with something heavy, lost, these big, restless bodies, even at this early hour roistering as hell and most of all loud, almost bafflingly open, like the sea at the opposite end of the street; but still, in those long muted lulls between pints, when the barman was skilfully rotating the glasses beneath the brass tap so the foam, those creamy clouds, laid itself slowly upon the black waters and was overlaid with hope, with con-solation, a beery firmament – then, in that profound silence, as if in melancholy, you could sense in the hands and eyes of these people something fantastical, mysterious, something that could be neither drowned nor spoken, something that drives writers to write, sailors to sail, like an unfathomable, unquenchable thirst that gnaws at you, that calls for another large glass of the dark stuff. I thought of home. I wanted to talk to somebody about it, when I had circled through all the secluded alleys, the cross streets, the roundabouts and cul-de-sacs of this coastal town, as if searching in the darkness on the street for something important, a precious souvenir from the road, the key to the house waiting for me at home far away across the sea. That night as I sailed on the high waves of granite, I know it was longing for home that carried me – I walked, I wandered, I searched for a harbour where I could hide myself; I saw the menacing sea, below, in front of the museum, in the canal by the monument to Christopher Columbus – it pounded and thundered among the colourful façades of the narrow little streets, the underpasses and squares, as if to warn those who were fleeing and to beckon to those who were hesitating, for we know, everyone is drowning – this was echoing somewhere like a refrain from the pubs. I could see the picture, I was calling it to mind, the canvas that had so strangely fascinated me on my visit to the Galway museum, now as I sat numb on the worn seat, my arms across my stomach so it wouldn't empty itself over my trousers, as the sea tossed us to and fro like air turbulence high in the clouds; the only thing that calmed me was the thought of that restful gallery light floating in the quiet, empty space; only once in a while, from somewhere far away, the ground floor or the lobby, did the murmur of children's voices drift in, or maybe it was only seagulls, their cries entering the gallery from the harbour, as somebody inaudibly opened the door, maybe came in and stood undecided in the lobby, wondering whether to look at the collection of old Galway boats, which were once used for fishing, or for escaping the Great Famine and death, or maybe he wanted to climb the long staircase to the third floor, to the dark and windowless wing of the gallery, and have a look at the painting *An Island Funeral* by Jack B. Yeats, which I was standing in front of at that very moment – who knows? No, the random visitor would certainly reconsider; the idea of death on that sunny morning, when it still hadn't rained

although somewhere out in the bay clouds were already moving, descending over the sea, was too hard for him, even if it only floated above the undulating surface like dissipated light, merely an intimation or suppressed memory; it alighted on him like the dark but unseen shadow of a thought, which would soon possess him, the lover who was still debating whether to move towards it, who would be unable to escape it even if he went to the end of the world; so the traveller shifted his feet, the soft rubber soles of his hiking boots or running shoes scraping menacingly on the waxed floor of the museum, giving him away; there was a squeaking noise, and that's when I saw it, the painting in the wide gilt frame, when the unknown visitor swiftly pivoted towards the exit, rescuing himself from the ominous, dark waves of thoughts, of memories, that would soon engulf him; below, in the big glass-walled foyer, from which the view opened on to colourful boats moored at the dock across the road, the random visitor, as he was leaving the gallery, glanced through the high glass wall and saw, as if already in the open air, a man sitting on the stern of a fishing boat – he wore a woollen cap and a yellow, sea-bleached oilskin, and in his left hand he was clenching a pipe, which he was trying to relight; the mute observer in front of the museum exit, caught before this great living painting, the most beautiful seascape he would ever see, maybe even then discovered a detail in this powerful picture, or maybe he would notice it only much later, in the now-faded memory, and then, like the echo of the seabirds' cries, the notion would strike him: he would see that the fisherman with the pipe, now similarly sensing something, was looking far out across the rolling sea, all the way to Mutton Light, which from there looked like a miniature model, a squat mushroom at the end of a long pier, where the brownish sea was already dipping and rising on the piles of enormous rocks that guarded the way to the last lighthouse in their world; both of them, the traveller in the shelter of the gallery and the old fisherman on his boat, by then could sense that the sea would soon be churning again, the wind chafing at it, quickening it, trying once more to lift it into the air, to take it to itself up in the sky and put on again its fallen mask, an image glinting on the surface of the sea. That's when I saw it, as I said, the painting in the wide gilt frame, when the unknown visitor below had already left the gallery and all that remained was the squeaking echo of his footsteps, the sharp sound of rubber soles, and maybe the trapped cries of excited gulls, the only thing that remains when we leave an island. I returned, exhausted and windblown, to the Hotel Meyrick. I was delighted and surprised to see Suzana, who I met in the reception area; I hadn't been expecting her until the next day; she was sitting in the lobby, buried in a wide, deep velvet armchair; I only just arrived – Clifden is lonely, like writing, is all she said; we understood each other. Her suitcase was still by her side; she looked tired from travelling by bus, serious but smiling none the less; I finished the text, she said, I didn't want to stay another night in the hotel in that abandoned train station. I'll be on the boat with you tomorrow. Of course, we understood each other. Clifden is already far away. She lifted herself out of the armchair and looked across the room, like a castaway on a raft; she was looking for an island, for land, so she could rest and quench her thirst. A man in a dark threadbare suit and a shimmering black bowtie, as if he'd just rushed in through the back door from a funeral, I thought – on the way from the grave to the hotel he must have lingered too long over his beer in the remote village pub adjacent to the cemetery's low, blackened stone wall, where funeral-goers and other mourners took shelter after leaving their grief behind earlier at the cemetery, to lighten their souls with the morning's first pint of Guinness; the tongues of the assembled black-suited company were soon loosened, but because five minutes to noon wasn't yet a decent time for singing, although those who rested beneath the stones overgrown with clumps of dry grass most likely could not see the mourners on the other side of the wall with sinful glasses in their hands, which might have led even the blessed and pure into temptation, their silent and sparkling but still turbid eyes, like silver sand in the waves, merely wandered around the room as if not knowing where they belonged, to which body the wounded soul should return, and so they were drifting somewhere beneath the old, low, black and smoky ceiling, somewhere over the shoulders, over the black hats, the grey coats, through the thicket of ruddy, warm, plump faces, to that faraway place, far out in the open sea, as if all these zealots, fanatical Christians and godless heathen at once, were still looking for that old single-masted boat that carries the coffin to the other side, to the place one can only travel to alone – so then, the man in the Sunday suit deftly placed two large glasses of beer between us, a particularly cold beer, is how the black raven put it, who for the rest of the evening flitted soundlessly high above the bar, watching for thirsty, weary or lonely travellers in the desert, who were sending him covert signals warily, guardedly and with exaggerated politeness, addressing him with minute gestures so as not to alarm or frighten this lordly bird who had just now perched on the spigots above the counter, cast in pure gold and polished to a sheen, which opened up beery firmaments; yes, yes, the bird would proudly flutter his wings, not blinking an eye, and just a few more long pauses in the conversation had to be endured,

during which the parched tongue desperately seeks a name for its lost soul like a wilting bunch of flowers in a vase of standing water, and then the velvet malt topped with a creamy crown was already melting slowly on the tongue, and Suzana and I soon resumed our conversation, talking the way people do when they say goodbye or have returned from far away, in melancholy, mysterious and somewhat elevated tones, when every word, smuggled across an invisible border, sounds binding and momentous, like scarce news from home.

We parked in the big car park for visitors, not far from the marked entrance where buses, too, had been stopping, only everyone had left by now; during the remainder of the trip, which by the clock had lasted barely more than half an hour, we had said nothing, which made me feel that we would never actually reach our destination. The storm – in fact, a cloud must have broken away, as if the darkest side of the sky had opened for a moment and above us the sky had wept, I thought later, but I had neither the words nor the will to say this to Gjini; mainly, I was hurt, and angry, too, that he had left me alone waiting in the car in the middle of a deluge, which, of course, out of politeness, and hospitable gratitude, too, I was now trying to conceal, but I couldn't hide all of it – the flood subsided for real only when we were driving again, changing eventually into a downpour and then dwindling to a drizzle, to bands of mist, which floated above the peat bogs and the bends in the road between the black valley overgrown with clumps of dry, golden grass and the steep hillside, which was already casting its shadow on the winding narrow road we had taken here. We had, indeed, caught no more sun on the second leg of the trip; we were gliding down the ever-narrowing gorge like drops of water in a funnel, into which the valley was slowly pouring itself; the only thing still shining on its fresh green body was the clear, late-afternoon blue, which slowly slipped into twilight and darkened in an instant when, in total silence, we drove through a sparse wood; and then a wonderful light, and I will probably never forget this moment, was suddenly in all its sharpness hovering above the black, rippling surface of the lake, as if it had burnished itself to a shine against the edges of the mountain cliffs around the valley and then, out of the pure, cold depths, had risen once more above the immortalized scene; I remember, as if it were now, that as I watched, but before I could take a picture, the light simply dissipated, as if it wanted to gently touch, to shine upon, something else, the way only our most fragile, most precious, but also most achingly beautiful memories are illuminated. In fact, the light that had then flashed in the sky merely caressed them with its mysterious grace – I still don't know any other word for what remained in my memory, for the great image soon faded in the darkness, so that almost nothing of that first impression, the initial innocent glance, remained with me except this indescribable and undepictable feeling. I'll explain later, Gjini said after changing his soaking shirt in front of the car, here you never know when you'll be drenched to the bone, he added and smiled, let's go, we're already late. We were walking with quick steps on the narrow, carefully raked gravel path that curved along the lake shore. The light, which had only shortly before imprinted itself on my memory, evaporated even before we reached the end of the walkway from the car park to the little bridge, for in those few minutes a heavy but somehow tidier, calmer rain had begun to come down again, pounding the lake, which was not yet fully visible; I could see only the low shore bordered with well-tended green grass, the water puckering in the pre-evening rain; the vast surface of the lake, meanwhile, was still obscured by tall reeds and long, undulating blades of yellowed grass; look, Gjini said, there it is – this is where you have the finest view of this wonderful manor.

We took a few more quick steps and hid beneath the great trees that lined the shore in a long allée on this side of the lake; that's when I saw it, too, the enormous manor, lonely, grand and aloof beside the lake, its back right up against the enormous back of a mountain, its slender turrets rising peacefully high above the water; but the observer could see at once that the turrets had not been placed there for the defence of the manor, although, to be sure, it was situated in an empty, lonely landscape where it might be easy prey for brigands or invaders; rather, the perceptive architect must have added them at the request of the tenants, to provide a vantage point, for they would certainly offer you a stirring prospect of wild but, for the sensitive human eye, also tranquil nature, I thought; everywhere you could feel the note of intensity, the carefully chosen composition and the endlessly changing light, as if everything here had been created with inspiration, with refined sensibility, and most of all, which you could sense right away: everything here is made from love and dedicated to memory, Gjini said.

This picture, the way the sea coast is portrayed, enchanting and suffused with death, as if you are literally standing in front of the gates to a new world, one you must go to alone, over the high white steps of the waves, as Ivo Andrić put it so succinctly in one of his sea tales, I said to Gjini later, when we were waiting in front of the ramp to board the hydrofoil, it's all somehow affected me, touched me deeply, the way I'm often moved when I encounter an unknown, foreign, different sea, I told Gjini, as if again and again I'm struck by the thought, an unanticipated realization, like the surprise a man feels when, for the first time, he has left his home and stands alone with himself on a remote, foreign, ominous coast, which instils in him the inexpressible feeling of being a traveller, and indeed, he can't find the words for what he sees in front of him; he is presented with something he knows only from the tales of the few who have returned, and returned, in fact, as foreigners, in black tailored suits with wild eyes and restless hands, and maybe even now, as I read these lines back to myself, somewhere on an unknown coast a foreigner is standing, a person who is leaving and will possibly return one day as a stranger, and he is wrestling with the thought that those who went too far were telling the truth, even if they didn't yet have the language to describe it and said only that the sea is not of one body, and perhaps the eternal voyager thinks, I said to Gjini, that all the many faces of the sea, which are immersed within it and hidden, its kaleidoscopic eyes, which paint strange pictures inside us, dark, azure expanses, a feeling of freedom, the call of faraway places but also the call of the end, are beyond his reach, submerged in an infinity about which he can know nothing. That's what the sea islands tell us through their poetics, Gjini said; what we are looking at, all this beauty in the rain (the storm was raging again), this is not the sea that you and I know, this is not the domain of our blessed, sweet and intoxicating Mediterranean trinity of sea, rosemary and red wine – here I have never once imagined, he said, that we were truly made of the same stuff as the summer; maybe so much the better, I whispered, mumbled under my breath, as I looked across the bay from the boarding ramp at the dark, windy, stormy coast, how it was leaning over us, we who were leaving, who were sailing away to the last islands of this world. The sea and the wind were tossing the hydrofoil to and fro, bearing it away like a discarded cigarette butt. I gazed fixedly out through the boat's round window, as it sank into the bottomless wavy line; I held my breath and shut my eyes a moment, until a black wave spat us out into the clear

again, and then the hydrofoil was sailing on the high crest of a foaming wave; we were carried off, far into the distance, as if flying, with nothing beneath us now to hold us back, to rock us into a safe harbour. The tolling of a bell – the sound was falling on the sea or rising from its depths like the echo of a village bell that perhaps had sunk to the bottom, and only its voice, muffled and refracted, had been caught by the wind and now drifted aimlessly above the waters, unable to find its way, to find its echo beneath the mighty cliffs, and in the breaking of the waves could only repeat the names of the dead and the drowned, sing dirges from the throats of the seabirds above the rocks that hunt for food in the shelter of the fog, I thought; we are bound to the world by the insatiable emptiness of hunger and the eternal search for a clear view, are like the birds and the bells, the drowned and the saved, as Primo Levi said. In this hollow and empty intermediate space, between the fury of the sea and the cracks in the sky through which a few rays of sunlight had escaped, which were shining on the tips of the

sharpened waves and with a single stroke could have sliced deep into the body of the hydrofoil, I knew we were about to sink, like prey in the belly of a mighty sea beast that would never spit us out again, never free us from its teeth; in this hollow intermediate space, neither in the air nor deep at the bottom, I heard only the whistling and twisting of iron, the crash of waves flooding the deck and muffled whispers, restrained gasping, guttural singing without meaning, the noises of unsettled stomachs, something between hunger, nausea and despair, the sounds that once perhaps developed into human language, something capable of reviving the memory of the first sea crossing to a yet unknown land, to the last islands of my world. It's not so bad really, Gjini said a while later, when he came down the steep and narrow steps from the boat's upper saloon; he spoke as if I had caught him in the middle of a thought, or in my own self-absorption and deepening sense of nausea, the ever clearer and more conscious feeling that I was becoming the prey of that treacherous seasickness and, to put it simply, in words I was afraid to utter, that I would soon be vomiting, that the infirmity would strike me as well – I had been smelling it in the air for a few minutes now, a stale acidic odour issuing from stomachs and from the plastic bags tourists were clinging to and hiding between their legs – Gjini's words, then, were calm and well-chosen, as if he had written them down in the notebook in his glove compartment or carefully dictated them to a typist, a highly skilled, trustworthy secretary, as he had once done in the editorial offices of Albania's national radio station, or behind the securely closed doors of the ministerial office he had climbed to after the fall of the regime and shortly before he'd emigrated for good; in other words, he was speaking as if the listener was by now thoroughly accustomed to the rhythm and, especially, the content of the narrator's story; I was stunned, Gjini said; that first meeting with Jane at the station was like an extraordinary and unconscious outburst of empathy, or for me at least it had to feel that way, Gjini continued in a measured, thoughtful voice – a kind of self-defensive reflex, maybe just a fleeting friendship, in fact, a forced alliance with no possibility of choice, but that came much later; then, at that first meeting at the bus station, and nobody could have known it yet, least of all Jane and me, what perhaps connected us was something I still think about now, something much deeper, hidden in all of us, a feeling of foreignness, of statelessness, and at the same time a strange and unfathomable need to be close to someone, Gjini said, although it was nothing more than a friendly invitation to take a short trip with her, hmm, Gjini said and once more lifted himself off the tall chair; he looked around the saloon; I turned my tired and heavy head, sleepy from the rocking on the rough sea and from nausea; Gjini was standing, arms and legs spread out, between the rows of tall, black, well-worn chairs like the captain of a sinking ship or like a foreigner, a pirate who has just taken the helm and saved us from the sea – saved the heads of all the tourists, with mobiles and tablets in their hands ready for a last SOS SMS or at least the confirmation of our location on Google Maps, to mark the point of the expected drowning, just in case, lest our deep, cold and undulating grave remain hidden and anonymous. After all, for many of us, all that remained was the still-latent thought, the cheap false comfort, that our virtual friends on social media would one day grieve for us, at least when they visited our abandoned profile, since what remains of us, they hope, will be saved on our virtual wall – photos, posts, known and unknown friends, links and likes, something that will be somewhere recorded for ever, if only a meagre eternity, but sadly, as I myself had at that moment discovered, there was no hope left for us, no net was reachable, for some time now we had been without a mobile signal; the murk, the fear and desperation that nobody would ever find us, was mixed with a feeling of disquiet and disappointment, a basic senselessness: we were going to drown, just like everyone before us, hungry and illiterate and nameless, who had once sailed these waters fleeing a great famine, weeping for the last trace of the beam from Mutton Light; we would be lost among the shipwrecks of old, castaways who had no chance to say goodbye or send an email, update our status or post one last selfie.

With no illusions of happiness, no desire for quick success or rapid advancement, or for a new beginning in a distant and foreign land, which for me was in every sense completely new, it was as if in those first days after I arrived, when I was living on the street, so to speak, I was a new-born child, speechless and anonymous, and that really is precisely how I was, since I had come here without a residence permit and, what's more, didn't know a single word of English, and even worse, you might say, said Gjini, which I understood only later, when I was no longer afraid I might die of hunger or, god forbid, have to go back, and had already learned a few crucial words, like how to ask where the toilet was if I didn't see a sign with an arrow or symbol – oh yes, I remember how in those first post-natal days I was entirely dependent for my survival on a language of symbols, which was the only one I understood, and that only barely – so when the culture shock passed, and that, too, was something that before then I had no clue even existed, and I no longer felt threatened – to be honest, it wasn't that I felt the Irish were particularly welcoming, let alone empathetic, but in a way they accepted me, or more precisely, they let me keep fighting, and I have to say that although it was a fair fight, it was also cruel and merciless, and it's still going on after all these years; I mean, I don't enjoy any obvious privileges here, but I'm not belittled either; still I have to admit that I have never noticed any indications of corruption even between themselves, he said; really, there have been lots of times when I had to go to the end of a long queue, but there was always someone who came behind me, nobody tried to push past me, or jump the queue, which is probably the only bright thing this dark nation inherited from their cruel English colonizers – law, hierarchy and the absolute prohibition of corruption in all public institutions, especially the schools and courts, which I later experienced myself the hard way, Gjini said, and in a sense, of course, that was something I myself had to learn, which is why I don't feel sorry for myself now or complain about my position; right after I arrived, even before I was working at the bus station, where for a few days I was living, you might say, because I didn't know anybody and didn't even know how to ask for help, Gjini said; so then, even before I got on my feet, through my own strong will and determination, I knew that hard work was the only way I would survive here, and now, as you can see, I work without a break, sometimes as much as fifteen hours a day if not more, Gjini said. His determined words, I felt, seemed to calm even the wind and the sea; the hydrofoil was now rising and dipping more steadily, the tourists had revived and found their second wind and now that the worst was over, somebody opened the door from the upper deck and the sea air, cool, clean and moist, rushed into the saloon. How are you today, Suzana? Gjini asked with a smile – she had just come down the steps to the saloon; better, much better, Suzana said with a sour smile, which betrayed both her nausea and a hint of worry about our fate, but now that the round windows were glistening with rays of sunlight refracted in the salt crystals on their thick glass – for the waves were becoming calmer and only some-times still reached the level of the saloon – we, too, with the sea, were calmer and more cheerful; this will make a beautiful photograph, I said and took a few pictures through the porthole with my telephone. The black sea, rolling in long and shallow swells, pleated and poured itself towards the horizon, where clouds were shredding themselves apart and a clear bottomless blue sky was already visible, shining inside the now even blacker, overexposed, porthole frame, like a painted image from an altar of grace and blessing. Fine, but . . . Gjini said – he was turning his telephone around in his hand and flicking through the photograph album; he would stop for a moment at a picture and compare it to the live image in the distance, as if he had doubts about the photo's truth, then return quickly to an earlier photo, somewhat in haste but with purpose, as if he was trying to say some-thing but couldn't find the right words; he wasn't ambling through the pictures, didn't look at them, peer at them; instead, I'd say he was racing through them, merely rummaging, as people used to do with old paper photographs in bound leather albums, as if he'd taken a big box of disorganized, tossed-together photos out of the sideboard and was turning them over, portraits and panoramas, to show them to some random viewer, a stranger unfamiliar with the connections between the relatives or the family tree or the chronology, which for him were utterly without meaning or beauty, who had no interest in questions about what happened first and what came later, which relative had left us or even who was missing from the official family portrait because their place in memory was yet to be won, their space in the family album was yet to be secured – but . . . he said, when on the rolling and swift-moving horizon there first appeared a still shadow on the sea, the shape, like a black-paper silhouette, of the islands; but, Gjini said, beauty is somewhere else, or maybe it doesn't exist at all, since you know I was born in the godforsaken mountains of the Balkans, a place hidden from human eyes, in a land where a single man had outlawed beauty and installed in its place an aesthetics without the beautiful, Gjini said, but despite the violence and the programmed ignorance, a feeling for the beautiful and the transcendent, despite the isolation, the total censorship, the empty galleries, closed churches, plundered libraries, and systemic unanimity, that is to say, despite the void, with no images of the beautiful at all, in a world of cheap didactic poetry, with stonemasons and housepainters fulfilling the cultural officials' state commissions, that is to say, after all of those things which I myself, of course, wanted to get away from, beauty, the soul, which is something I understand only now, was nevertheless kept safe. It never died, it shines somewhere else, like hope, Gjini said as the boat's horn let out a short blast; in our country, religion was against the law, love, from time immemorial, had been an arrangement between old men plotting the fate of their descendants and the principle of hope was unknown to us, but in the forgetting itself, in the suppression and the menacing prohibition, the meaning was preserved, which is something I only learned here, Gjini said as the horn's blare startled the seagulls sitting on the black reefs; its sound, mixed with the cries of the awakened birds, and Gjini's words, too, would still be echoing somewhere high above the island, even long after we had left the harbour behind, but the water in the bay only sighed indifferently; behind the long, wide and deep breakwater, the dark substance, heavy and tense, wheezed like a trapped ghost, which at any moment might leap across the pier and escape, taking with it the boats, the few tourists and the harbour crew in their yellow oil-skins, but then, once the strong gale abated that had been driving it against the pier where we had just docked, the tamed watery mass was momentarily calm again. The dark surface, sliced at the edges by the hydrofoil's white furrow, now glistened in the sun, which made long shadows over the sparse houses on the other side of the bay as it slipped slowly above the ridge of the Aran Islands. We moved gradually in a queue towards the narrow exit, radiant with the clean white light that after the storm was gleaming from the hydrofoil's white hull; looking through the opening, I could feel the boat's unstable, fragile and rocking shell, which we now departed in silence, as if we could feel it, hear it, groaning, tensing and relaxing under the mighty, invisible force of the sea, which like cosmic background radiation was, unthinkingly, pressing down on, eating away at and breaking apart the island, which once had been the last tangible trace and refuge for all who were sailing far away, too far away.

I waited for him beneath a tree; tiny glistening raindrops now pricked the water's surface, sinking into its dark-grey depths, and all was quiet and palpably still around the lake, like a long, peaceful sleep after a watchful night; muddled heaviness and endless weariness, a feeling of stony patience, had settled over the gorge, and now only translucent threads were dripping off the tree leaves, and every so often a calyx would tip over and spill into the late hour of the late-afternoon stillness of the world. The cold and, especially, the distance that lay behind me – here, I felt, was a few steps too far – enveloped me, spoke to me in the cunning voice of the wily serpent: enter, stranger, stay with me, the mask of death dressed up as a gorgeous landscape whispered in my ear. Here I might have the peace I need for writing, which I have travelled so far to find, I was thinking, or maybe after a few days of solitude I would go crazy here, the thought came to me. I was startled by the sound of a splash and a muffled cry, echoing through the gorge; convinced that someone had dived into the cold lake, I ran my eyes across the water, looking for a swimmer; by now he must have come to the surface and be pounding and ploughing the water with his strokes, which I certainly would have heard, but the lake remained still, as if its heavy lid of water was hermetically sealed. I left the shelter of the trees, took a step closer to the water and kneeled down, when again there came a cry, redoubled by an echo from somewhere far away on the opposite bank; I lowered myself over the surface of the lake; the glowing tip of the cigarette I had lit moments before, which was pinched between the fingers of my right hand, suddenly and unexpectedly touched the water and went out without a sound, the flame swallowed by wetness; the last trace of my presence here, by which an observer on the opposite bank could watch me even from far away, had drowned; sound travels far over water, I thought and held my breath, again listening intently; it was as though I heard someone breathing deeply, a heart beating against a thick wall and, again, something like the gentle, rhythmic, broad and practised strokes of powerful arms, a swimming that neither disturbed nor rippled the surface; only concentric circles were spreading out, all around, evenly spaced waves lapping against the banks and breaking on my submerged hand, around which evenly spaced, fragile rings of water were expanding; for a moment, before Gjini appeared in a freshly soaked shirt, I felt that maybe this was a speech I didn't know, a language transmitted by waves on water like Morse code, except that the water was communicating not just letters and words but also sighs, rhythm, silence, the beating of a heart, fear, love and death – not just meaning, then, but also sense. He looked like he had just emerged from the lake; he was standing in the grey shadow of the line of trees, soaked through and out of breath, wiping his glasses on the hem of his wet black shirt, but he was again cheerful, quick and obligingly open; I understood that we were again running late, there'd been enough waiting and somewhere a bell was tolling for me, but now I was the one who had to stop; I heard a swimmer, somebody dived into the lake, in this weather – did you run into anyone? I said after we took a sharp turn off the path that curved around the lake; the manor must be far behind us now, if my senses don't deceive me, I thought as I struggled to keep up with my guide. We were rapidly climbing a winding forest trail; at the edges of the conifers and the dense, though squat, broadleaf trees, which were leaning in the direction of the hill on which we, like the trees also bent over, were now marching in long strides – high up, then, at the folded margins of the trees, the tenuous, almost translucent grey light of the dwindling day still hovered, while below, in the embrace of the plants and in the sky's distant reflection in the shrouded lake, the planetary twilight was already rolling in – a light by which it would be impossible now to read but also a lamp by which the skilled writer would not yet have put down his pen – I knew that if I had been following a map, I would surely now be lost, but Gjini knew the terrain we were entering more and more determinedly, the landscape into which we were disappearing.

Jane, Gjini said, Jane was standing right here by the road the first time I took her on those long drives of ours, which somehow I soon took as my own – he was telling me as we drove back to the city from the manor. Early the next morning, just a day after our chance encounter, which later turned out not to have been so accidental, you know, Gjini said, for the simple reason that, presumably, she must have seen

me arriving or leaving the station with my car, at least once – I was driving a Toyota back then, too, you know, he said as we slowly snaked our way along the road, past the peat bogs, which I merely intuited must be there, since it was already completely dark, a hard, deep darkness that stretched across the landscape, which I could see only in the narrow yellow beams of the headlights when the wipers wiped away the thick little raindrops on the windscreen – the next morning, then, as we were leaving the city, she told me she had come to Connemara because she was searching for her lost home; I'm an American, but my father was born around here, Jane said, but he never asked questions about it, he only told me he was a war orphan, she said; at the end of the Second World War some friendly nuns put him on a ship – he was five years old, Jane said, and he travelled from these shores to Canada with other Irish orphans and immigrants, specifically, to Nova Scotia, where he was greeted at the dock by an elderly lady in a warm coat and a gentleman in a black hat, Jane said; sadly, I never met them. That was enough for my father, she said and repeated it many times, Gjini said. I wasn't born here myself, I said to Jane, as I drove the car at a slow speed; I know, she said; I suppose you could see it right away, I said; no, she said, not see it, hear it; I heard it right away, Jane said, Gjini said. So do we have a travel plan? I asked Jane, since she was letting me drive as if on a Sunday outing, but I had things to do, Gjini said.

I felt a chill beneath my sodden sweater, and also fever, fatigue and saturation, I was full of sensations, of baffling impressions that pushed their way into my consciousness like pictures in a disorganized photo album; I couldn't gather my wits and concentrate on the drive, on the story or at least on the slow and monotonous rhythm of the windscreen wipers. I was sure I was going to fall asleep when somewhere outside I noticed a flame, a spark, as if somebody in the night had lit a cigarette; it was definitely on the other side of the car's misted windows; I looked out through a blot, a wound, which opened into the night – I remember it was where I had been resting my nodding head – and looking through it now, I saw a flame flapping low above the ground in the hollow night, the wind pushing it down and fanning

it, a white serpent's tongue of smoke streaming across the blind land as if lit from within; I quickly shifted my head and leaned my forehead on the glass for a longer, sharper view, and then, in the dark distance, another flame lashed out, and between the two fires I noticed a third – look, look, Gjini, I said, as suddenly the whole earth was burning, was rising in flames; I heard crackling noises, and gasping, too, like someone suffocating, somewhere deep beneath the surface. But the fire, the burning earth, the magical radiance, illuminated nothing around us, who were still moving slowly towards the city, as if it was only smouldering and unable to ignite, as when a star implodes – a celestial light, I thought later, which after billions of years of travelling through the darkness has here, for a moment, found its last reflection, a ray from the universe that brings somebody joy. Could you drop me at the diving tower, please? I'll go on foot from there – I can use the walk, I said when I revived a little, woke up from the half-sleep that had anaesthetized me during the ride; yes, of course, Gjini said; Jane, too, when we came back to the city, that's the same place I would always drop her off, too, by the diving tower; a few times I remember when, after we'd been driving around all day in the car or just walking in the countryside, usually by the sea – she loved the bluffs, the high cliffs with the waves crashing far below; yes, that's something you still have to see, he said, I'll definitely try and organize it – yes, so, late at night, when we got back and had already said our goodbyes, he said, Jane would say, I'm going for a swim. I was surprised, of course, and tried to talk her out of it – not now, Jane, it's late, it's raining and the waves are rough, I'd tell her, and it's night, there's nothing you can see now, Gjini said; the lighthouse, Mutton Light, is shining there in the distance, Jane said; I can see its beam in the darkness, so you go on now, I'm going to have a swim; I'll meet you here in the morning – good night, Gjini, Jane said; good night, Jane, Gjini said.

We had climbed to somewhere near the top of the steep hill and it suddenly got brighter, just as it did here, on the diving tower, where I was recalling the trip – in the distance the light from the city was shining beneath a dark and cloudy sky, while the glow of the street lamps illuminating the coastal promenade disappeared in the black sand and washed-up clumps of rotting seaweed; I sat down on the highest platform and tried to light a cigarette, as I looked in vain in the windy evening for Mutton Light, which was similarly perched on top of its reef, solitary and invisible like me, immersed in the stories of others who had sailed past in the fog; as soon as we had wriggled out of the shelter of the broadleafs and conifers, which at the end of the forest trail were now at a full uphill slant, an azure blue unveiled itself above us, stretching above a ridge a few hundred yards higher, where there was nothing but shimmery bare rock strewn with sharp scree and overgrown with sparse reddish grass; I straightened up and felt pain in my lower back and a sharpness in my lungs as if those bent and flattened trees had grafted themselves into me during the climb – hurry up, hurry up, there's still a lot to see, Gjini said; he had gone far ahead even before I could turn my eyes away from the lake, which lay in the distance below like a miniature painting in the palm of an enormous stony hand. The turreted manor, which abutted the hill

from where I surveyed my surroundings, I could not see – it was too deep beneath the cliff; Gjini, meanwhile, had disappeared from sight; slowly please, go slower, I said under my breath and with trembling step made my way up the path, I remembered.

The gleaming cloud above the city was carried out to sea by a wind that came up suddenly from the other side, the mist shining like a gas lamp hung high beneath the shrouded dome of the sky; the light, white and pure, floated slowly away from the coast and into the distance, but, contrary to the rules of perspective, the distant gleaming ball was not getting optically smaller; in my eyes, as I watched it from the diving tower, where the wind was blowing stronger and stronger, it stayed the same; travelling across the dark, undulating seascape, palpable, inspiring, and terrible, it might have been merely an optical illusion or a clever *trompe-l'œil* painting, an unusual, ingenious accent, a marker between the sky and the earth, like the grave in the remote wilderness Gjini and I had visited that day, which contained a hidden message and meaning, it occurred to me as, lingering there for some time, I lay on my back on the highest platform of the diving tower, gazing up at the starless sky; he was standing by the mound of dark-red earth, which, in the little light there was when I finally caught up with him, when I finally found him, had dwindled to nothing, since in order to find him by that grave, marked only by an old stone cross, I first had to go down into a hollow at the end of a steep path, which was even more crooked than the one on the other side, where we had climbed the slope. I had heard the sound of mountain streams, of water rushing from every side into the deep and narrow defile between the foggy slopes, where this solitary grave lay next to the dangerous, but beautiful, path, I was thinking not long afterwards, as we followed it down to the tranquil lake below, where all these streams converged. I could already feel the chill and fever that would wash over me much later, on the ride back to the city, when I had trouble breathing or focusing even for a moment, but when I walked up to Gjini, who was wiping drops of water off the cross with his hand, I couldn't find the right words to tell him and said nothing – the fever subsided only now, as I lay on the diving tower under the stars, with that *trompe-l'œil* painting in the distance – Jane would always come here first, he said; it makes sense to begin the story here, Jane said, Gjini said, and so be it; let's go, he said, we're running late. Jane told me later, after she bought a sandwich from my improvised stand at the bus station – which is how I was earning the money to pay for school, and for my own daily sandwich, he had told me that morning when he picked me up in his red Toyota and we left on our trip to Kylemore Abbey – that she had missed her bus and needed a ride; I wouldn't like to lose another day, Jane said, Gjini said; I only have a few more days for travelling, then I need to get ready for the long journey home. I remember she had been coming to the station for a few days in a row; she always arrived early, bought coffee from the machine, and then, with the plastic cup in her hand, would stand outside the door and smoke a cigarette, slowly, taking her time, while I was setting up my stand; naturally, we noticed each other, how could we not? – we were virtually the only ones in the waiting area at that hour; the city and regional buses were just starting to arrive and, I should add, the few people who got off them were, I think, going to hospital or to a specialist's surgery for consultation; at least that's what it looked like to me when they would simply exit the bus at the stop outside, slowly and too cautiously, and then right away disappear into the morning streets – and it was usually raining – without ever stepping into the foyer. So I would expect my first customers at seven o'clock – although I'd already been there since six – which is when the school buses arrived and, more importantly, according to the schedule, when the morning intercity buses would leave in every direction, to Clifden and, mainly, to Dublin, Gjini said, so it was my chance to make my earnings for the day; as a vendor, I was loud, friendly and fast, and I knew that in those couple of hours before nine, when most of the buses left the station, I had to make my money, and I have to say I was successful, said Gjini; the travellers on those long morning bus trips had an ample supply of my sandwiches, but from then until twelve o'clock, when I would quickly pack up my stand and race off to classes, it was mostly quiet – I hardly sold anything except a few bland cheese sandwiches left over from the morning rush – so in the time before I left I could read in peace, and I read a lot, anything I could lay my weary hands on, you might say, but mostly, of course, I read the morning newspapers and science magazines, which I could take for free off the racks of the news-stand in the bus station; I was good mates with the news dealer, he said; I would always bring him a tuna sandwich – on the house, of course – and he let me borrow tons of reading material, he said; in fact, that's how I learned to read and speak English, from newspapers and magazines, and after only a few months I was able to learn from books; then I passed the English exam and, for the second time in my life, entered university; when I met Jane, it was in the middle of that stressful, precarious period in my life, when I was wandering the rainy streets on sleepless nights, full of doubt and wondering if I should stay or leave, Gjini said.

At times, when an invisible breeze suddenly shifts the drawing paper on my worktable in front of an open window, or a random gust of wind turns a page in an open book during my afternoon drowsiness, it occurs to me that this same wind will eventually, after its long journey across the Atlantic, touch land again right here, beneath these cliffs, Jane said; how I wish sometimes I could sit for hours and hours – which, in fact, are coursing through me, inaudibly – sit motionless in front of an empty sheet of paper all day until night comes, and travel with the Gulf Stream, walking on the waves, as in some tangible, true dream, where in the end I touch these cliffs and shatter on the rocks in the waves, in the roar and thunder, which perhaps I am actually remembering, or maybe this earliest memory, the source of my inspiration, is something I merely invented, pictured in my imagination, so I would have somewhere to go, an escape from my own oblivion, Jane told me, Gjini said as we slowly climbed the steep, windswept plain. The initially wide, gravel-strewn trail, which had been twisting up the slope between low, grey stone walls like the antediluvian

serpent, now, somewhere halfway to the top, squeezed itself up against a wall and entered some prehistoric remains, a newly rescued ruin, I remember; without speaking, as if the booming, ever stronger gales were scattering all our words, we arranged ourselves in a hunched-over, compact queue, taking high, long steps from stone to stone, our faces turned to the crumbling path to be sure we didn't slip, didn't escape gravity and drop into the thundering void between sea and sky. The wind was blowing with ever greater power, pounding us from above and from the left, where from deep below the sea foam and fog were rising up and I heard sounds of breathing, gasping, sputtering. A mighty force was driving the high waves towards the overhanging rock face on the opposite side, somewhere I couldn't yet see, and pushing them on to the sharp, blackened rocks and through crevices, dizzyingly high, to the tops of the precipitous cliffs, where the Atlantic's force subsided and the waves disintegrated in the wind. The icy, salty mist fell like an eternal rain over the bitter, cracked and washed-out landscape, which was covered in scree and yellowish grass. Shyly and respectfully, I glanced from the corner of my eye at the grey sky dark with roiling clouds, which had risen from behind the cliff – it was like those old photographs on glass, with mercury stains in the sky and the contours of the overexposed landscape below in sepia – and stepped over the stone wall and started running, chest out, towards the wind. I stumbled my way across the big flat rocks abraded by wind, water and salt; I photographed their lines and cracks, as if I was standing on the hand of a dead giant; nothing was left in the stone but signs, the curves of lifelines, fingerprints and imprints, which now spoke only to the unhearing sky. In the distance, just a few quick strides ahead – or so it would have seemed to me if not for the deafening wind, which carried and lifted the waves up to the clouds, from the great wound, the great gash, cut deep in the island's body – the sea was churning in the distance, which I wanted to be closer to; distances, I sensed, were now within my reach, I could touch them, peer into them, as if into a tremendous dream, and not be lost, but I didn't dare take one step more; I just stood there, as if that mighty hand had grabbed me and was holding me back, a palpable caution watching over me; it occurred to me that I was crossing my own lifeline, which would end right here, on the edge of a foggy and thunderous cliff; I lifted my telephone in the air and made a short video. A few times we had planned to visit these bleak and windy yet fascinating islands, as Jane described them, but we never quite succeeded, Gjini said; twice, I remember, we came to the harbour very early in the morning, when the sea was still calm, was bathed in the orange light of early morning, but even before we could board the boat, the weather took a sudden turn for the worse, which is normal here, so it was too risky to sail, or the evening forecast looked doubtful and unpromising for the trip back, which meant we would have had to stay on the island and wait for good weather, which, of course, I couldn't afford to do back then – I had to work to pay for school, for my flat, for books, and not least of all had to put something away, too, since, as you know, somebody's always waiting for you somewhere,

Gjini said; so after each of these day trips of ours, which usually extended late into the night, Gjini said, the next day, or even the next few days, I needed to work hard to make up for lost time, although, to be honest, I never burdened Jane with these problems, and, I'm not sure, but Jane was maybe even quite wealthy, since she could afford so many trips to Europe; she would tell me about her trips to Belgium and how she had travelled all over France, and she gave me a particularly thorough account of her Balkan rambles, as she put it; she went by train from Vienna to Zagreb and Budapest, and she even mentioned Sarajevo, which I found especially interesting – that might also have been why we became so close and so quickly confided in each other; but, despite her study and research trips (which is how she talked about them), for which she undoubtedly needed money although I never really asked her how she earned it, Gjini said, well, despite all that, I never charged her mileage or per diems, Gjini said and resolutely lifted three fingers high into the air; at once we had a new round of Guinness at our table. We were sitting there, weary and windblown, on tall, heavy bar chairs of solid wood, leaning on the edge of a table crammed with glasses; this is the only pub on the island and, of course, for miles around, dear tourists, said the waiter, Martin; call me Martin, he said and laughed out loud through ragged teeth, which were the colour

and odour of dark beer, as with sorrowful and quivering eyes he counted the empty glasses; then he withdrew behind the bar and pulled at the golden tap handles skilfully, patiently and coolly. The beer slowly filled the tall, gleaming glasses, but Martin was looking at something far away, had wandered out through the low, narrow window opposite the bar, right next to the door that had only rarely been opened that day and maybe, after we, too, had sailed away on the last hydrofoil, would never be opened again. The old, low door of the only pub on the island and for miles around would one day be opened one last time on to the island, and the last fisherman would leave to search for his soul, Martin perhaps added on to the sorrowful poem he was unconsciously honing and revising somewhere within himself; he still watched the seemingly immutable and eternally unchanging scene in the harbour, just a stone's throw away; he saw the long breakwater, which had very likely been constructed when he was still a child; he probably didn't remember that any more – since I'm not so very old yet, he thought, even as he felt betrayed by his shaking hands, bad teeth and deeply scored weather-beaten cheeks, which in the past few days, or maybe months, or, god forbid, years, had been strangely drooping, sunken, he thought, as if for decades an invisible weight had been lodged beneath his tongue, a sort of dry substance black as bile, like numbness, like a heavy, hard-wearing stone, an unfathomable perseverance, a newcomer might say, a painful

expectation that produces an unparalleled thirst, a thirst that can never be quenched, the thought came to me when the glasses were filled to the brim and only a cold dew ran over the brim and down Martin's fingers; he turned his heavy eye away from the musings that had so often taken him over the bay, and again he must have certainly thought, even before he decisively picked up the glasses, with no danger of spilling even the least drop, his hand now steady once more, steadied by his gaze, which darted across the houses lit by the sun's last rays, standing in a row down by the bay, his own house among them, for as soon as he turned his eye away from his sorrowful musings, Martin must certainly have thought, must have affirmed to himself, that is where I come from, this is where my house stands, next to the church, right behind the wall of the cemetery, where nobody has been buried for a long time, since there are not many of us, you know, fewer and fewer, so people seldom die, he smiled to himself bitterly and with firm step walked over to the corner, where three silent men sat at a table full of empty glasses; they were spitting images of each other, with the same veiled look in their eyes, the same bitter weight under their tongues, certainly neighbours, maybe even brothers, who in the evening would open up the door and hold it for each other in the only pub on the island and for miles around, but nobody now was yet thinking of being the first to stand up and go out into the late afternoon light, which was getting darker in the harbour, where the last hydrofoil of the day waited to depart. We knew we had to catch it.

A little later that same spring I travelled to Belgium, for the second time in the space of only a few months. I remember it was the time of year when, at home, a hard-crusted snow, almost last year's snow, was still on the ground in less sunny places and along the edges of the pine and beech woods, but here you already sensed the increasing nearness and growth of the sun as it was diffused in an ever warmer atmosphere. Despite the cold wind, which was blowing low above the large oval square in front of the central Brussels railway station, where I had arrived by tram a little too early, the thought again crossed my mind from somewhere as I slowly smoked a cigarette, standing apart from traffic and the morning rush, that the low ruffled clouds, which seemed to be lying motionless above the roofs of the tall, monumental buildings that loomed above the street on every side, would soon break apart. I could see them in the tall and slender windows, which were discreetly recessed into the façades and extended all the way down to the wide entrances just above the wide-laned streets. From inside, the windows offered a view of the vast Brussels sky even as they blocked the eyes of the unconsecrated, of random passers-by, from peering into the discreetness of the commercial, financial and political institutions that lived their secluded and long, but barren, lives in sunny refuge. In the gleaming, darkened glass sealed in a metal grid of heavy frames, as I slowly smoked my cigarette that windy morning, I watched the reflection, the playful dance of forms, of light and dark, just as people had once done in the shadowy naves of Gothic cathedrals, and hoped that the sky really would soon break apart above me, and when the office workers, the secretaries with their big leather laptop bags and the account executives in dark skirts with tablets in their hands had taken off their heavy horn-rimmed reading glasses, logged out of the network one last time, and left their too-tight black shoes beneath their desks in the panopticon, they would fling open the tall windows and heavy oaken doors so the big, thick, sun-suffused clouds could enter the darkened interior, the same clouds I now saw merely in reflection. But on this side of the mirage, life flowed on, if only in accordance with its firm but never fully codified principles. The square in front of the station, across which that cold, low wind was swirling, and along with it a legion of office workers in dark, identically tailored coats and white shirts, was paved in a pattern of white and black trapezoidal tiles and completed architecturally by imaginative rows of identical pillars painted in black and white, which were joined in an ellipse at the top by a wide circumferential ring, thus playfully underscoring the meaning of the otherwise empty, although transitional and ephemeral, yet connective, space, which the railway station symbolized, Pavel told me a little later when, with paper cups of coffee in our hands like the vast majority of the passengers on their morning commute to work, we boarded the express train to Ghent. This is a lonely but intense city, Pavel said; you're all the time making compromises; I feel how exhausted I am but, on the other hand, I know I could never live anywhere else; you soon get used to the intensity; it's easy to lose yourself in the illusion of multiculturalism and the charm of difference, Pavel said, as the train hurtled past the ravaged and degraded suburbs. The city is constantly expanding; middle-class and working-class districts disappear overnight, so to speak, in deep construction pits excavated by financial speculators and anonymous investors, all of it in collusion with local politicians and under pressure from the multinationals, and it's obliterating the image of the landscape, relentlessly, and here on the ruins, in the dust and mud that have blotted out the former streets and squares and courtyards, and especially in the endless, nameless construction dumps, where they haul worn-out furniture, broken windows, abandoned toys, scorched enamel pots, shabby wooden flooring, quilted blankets and flattened pillows, toothless combs and hairbrushes for unemployed housewives and housekeepers and their healthy children, floral wallpaper, the torn-off covers of paperback books, scribbled-over maths and foreign-language workbooks for the lower levels of state schools, copies of marriage licences and birth certificates, and cheap colour reproductions of Dutch Old Master paintings, which hang in guarded, climatized museums and galleries where the evicted former residents probably never set foot – here, then, Pavel said, a new language is being born, forged from an explosive mix of forgotten and translated tongues, from such material as abandoned rubbish heaps and big investments. I remember a few years ago, when I was starting the first term of my lectureship, I was frantically looking for a cheap but suitable bedsit, which, of course, had to be as close as possible to a metro stop on a line with a connection to the central railway station, since there was no way I could afford to live in the centre, so before the

semester break was over and I had to start teaching in earnest in the department, I walked all round the suburbs with a Google map I'd printed out and lists of circled streets and house numbers where people had rooms to let. This was before the financial crisis hit – which in our country we were just starting to hear some timid whispers about – so housing prices were still sky high, which meant rents were, too. Every day I went further out, to the distant edges of the city, but rents and utility expenses were nearly the same everywhere. I was by myself and didn't have any major luggage, so to speak, just a suitcase and a laptop, so I could afford to move often and fast, Pavel said as the express train sped across a high overpass, then split away from a crowded junction with many interlacing tracks; now we were travelling towards Ghent on just a two-track line, along which a cluster of standardized one-storey terraced houses stood in seeming isolation. It was in just such a house, in one of the many monotonous developments around here, that I found my first rented room, in an attic, but I never stayed anywhere more than a few weeks; I moved from development to development, living virtually out of my suitcase, and nowhere did I find peace; you see, I was looking for a sense of home, of permanence, but you don't get that here; I had the feeling, the moment we were rumbling past, that to judge by their back gardens, which came right up to the tracks, the houses had long been deserted; the windows and doors, with gates to a central courtyard, were all closed, the shutters bolted and the blinds rolled all the way down; on the narrow plots, separated by unpainted, dilapidated fences, the grass was tall and bent and strewn with rusting debris, broken swings, snapped washing lines, beat-up garden sheds and rusty satellite antennas on tilted poles, but mainly it was covered in numerous derelict or discarded bicycles, which certainly nobody had ridden for a long time, either to the city or on the empty roads that went through fields and rolling meadows, where enormous and, that morning, quite motionless wind turbines rose into the sky. It was as though everything had stopped for a moment; the people must have recently moved out, and in a hurry, I thought, perhaps they had to flee, or maybe they were just sitting there immobile, which Pavel confirmed, since he had lived here for a while; all of us dozed off for a long time, Pavel said; we sat frozen in front of our televisions, expecting that our stupor, our unemployment and debts would eventually disappear, would melt away like the snows of yesteryear under the threat of global warming; after all, experts and pundits from various backgrounds, and especially the television presenters, who we are obliged to trust, must know what they're talking about when for twenty-four hours a day, seven days a week, they warn us about an invisible, inaudible, hollow and empty but terrible and pernicious epidemic, which purportedly, and this is true, erupted first in the form of a ravenous but seemingly benign fever on the American financial markets and then, albeit slowly, spread across the Atlantic through weakened stock markets and credit agencies, eventually infecting the entire globe with the deadly virus of doubt, fear and mistrust – our country, too, of course, Pavel said, and, of course, I agreed with him. The ones who survived the first outbreak called this new epidemic a financial crisis, and the diagnosis was accepted; the symptoms varied, but the methods of treatment were more or less the same everywhere. For its despairing, disgruntled and depressed viewers, television recommended lots of rest, organic herbal remedies with proven tranquillizing effects, shopping at clearance sales, better management of personal finances, and relaxing amusement by watching entertaining programmes, but especially and most importantly, patience, since everything eventually passes and the sun comes out after the rain, certainly next year if not before; meanwhile, for governments and countries, the spin doctors prescribed primarily reforms, restructuring, and a long course of austerity to be taken in large doses, for in their experience this was the only successful, and officially certified, medicine. Yes, Pavel said, as if he could read what I was thinking in my distant gaze and eloquent silence; yes, this insidious and incurable disease, which has got into our souls and our houses – it's what my students are asking me about today; they're deeply worried, and they also feel personally affected when they realize that, at the moment, and probably long into the uncertain

future, nobody really cares any more about their sincere commitment to the humanities, so they feel fundamentally useless, superfluous, which is what they hear every day from their older colleagues, from politicians, from professors and economists, but here there is actually a profound misunderstanding, the paradox of our ailing world, since all these professors, analysts and decision-makers should be their biggest allies, in a fellowship of tradition and academic alliance, for all of them, both the ones who are studying and the educated élite who decide our fates, belong to our common and indivisible humanistic tradition, an ideal, as my students tell me, that must not be made subject to the shady deals of conmen. You know, Pavel said, when the express train was stopping, as it insistently put on its brakes and the passengers, especially the office workers with their big briefcases, who had already tossed their paper cups and crumpled newspapers into the waste-paper bins, and the students with their backpacks and tablets in their hands, that is to say, all of us, even before the train had fully stopped, were standing up and starting towards the doors – that was when Pavel said, you know, I feel that something is going to have to change, that one morning people will simply have to object, will once and for all have to stand up and occupy the streets and squares and parks and demand that their dignity be respected; my only fear is that I don't know when and where it will end; I don't know what to tell them, my students, I mean; they know that I'm on their side, but I don't have any answers either, we're all still dancing around questions like what means are permissible and what is really the goal; now nothing and no one can excuse anyone any more, and every choice has already been made in advance or imposed on us, Pavel said. Should we defend ourselves, or should we attack? Are we the ones on trial, or the ones who pass judgement? – this, too, is something students are asking today, because, you know, they all want to know, and, if nothing else, that gives me comfort, Pavel said after we'd pushed our way to the front of the crowd and run through the train station's narrow underpass on to the bright, broad street.

I'll never be able to feel at home in this country, and I'll never understand these people, Gospođa Spomenka[1] said and dropped the cigarette she had been smoking into a tall coffee cup full of butts stained with her red lipstick; really, I never will, she said again and lit another cigarette. The formalism, the bureaucracy – it'll kill me; her words floated up on the bluish smoke to somewhere beneath the high ceiling of her office. We had met in the corridor when Pavel's seminar ended and then, as soon as we found our former common tongue, the language all three of us spoke, we'd retreated to her office, although I'm not sure we perfectly understood each other. For seventeen years I've been trying to tell them, these dutiful students who listen and look at me with their big wide eyes and probably interpret everything their own way, and how could they not? Gospođa Spomenka said and

1 The Serbo-Croatian title *Gospođa* (meaning *Mrs* or *Madame*), when used as here, with only a first name, implies a certain deference mixed with friendliness. (*Translator*)

suddenly stood up; just look, she said, raising her voice as she dropped a thick binder on the little coffee table – go on, look, maybe you'll understand what I'm talking about since you deal with literature for god's sake, she said, and you're also from our part of the world, she said. Pavel stood up and hastily shut the window, although the office was already filled with thick smoke; you see, we're not allowed to smoke indoors, not even here, not for a few years now, and we shouldn't be too loud either, Pavel said, picking up the papers that had tumbled out of the binder on to the old stone-tiled floor. And this is what they call academic freedom, Gospođa Spomenka said; we crouch in our offices like terrified mice, it's a disgrace for the university; I had a completely different upbringing, you know – I come from a place where literature used to mean something, Gospođa Spomenka said and checked the clock; I still have three minutes before my seminar and I'm always a minute late – although I was called on the carpet because of those few seconds, but I'm not giving in; they won't touch me; you know how it is, she said and pulled a book off a dusty shelf; look, I don't know what it's like now where you live, since I don't keep in touch with that region, she said, her hand shaking as she tapped the long ash tip into the cup, from which a dense whitish smoke was now rising; well, to be honest, even though I teach literature written in all the languages of our single cultural space, I've never had any real contact with your language or its literature, Gospođa Spomenka said; well, your friend Pavel has told me something, and I have to say it sounds interesting, but no offense, it would be easier to discuss it over a glass of decent brandy, don't you think? I know a good café in Antwerp where you can get real slivovitz; true, the owner's a little *Šiptar*,[2] nice enough, but what do you expect? They're the ones, along with the blacks and Asians, who are running things more and more these days in Antwerp, just as the Jews once did – you probably know that the Jewish gem dealers used to be a big local attraction, but nowadays the people with the money are eccentric designers and anorexic models, who sell themselves to the multinationals, which is why the

2 A derogatory term for Albanians (*Translator*)

city is losing its identity, becoming soulless – but that's fine with me, since we foreigners are welcome here, no one's upset by us, there's no nationalism; I've had more than enough of that, and I've gone through too much to worry about it now; I've had enough of that Balkan mentality, as I'm sure you understand; you really should come visit me, Gospođa Spomenka said; isn't that right, Pavel? she added with a smile and a wink to Pavel, who was carefully pouring water into the smouldering cup with the cigarette butts; they've put smoke detectors everywhere and they make this awful wail when they're set off, Pavel said as Gospođa Spomenka was lighting our cigarettes; well, what did I want to say? Oh right, I still believe there's only one literature, one great literature, or there isn't any at all; all those small-language literatures – that's never interested me; it's probably the same today in your country, I don't know, but undoubtedly you are interested, and personally affected, too, otherwise you wouldn't have come here, and come so far, to tell us your little stories; you want to share your sadness with foreigners who can barely understand what you're talking about; in the past, our great writers didn't need that; they had a big country and, most of all, they had a language everybody understood, said Gospođa Spomenka and got up quickly from her chair, her eyes taking in the crowded, smoke-filled, dark office, the last one in the alcove at the end of the corridor; you know, the students really do work hard, but they only study because they think they'll get some practical use out of this minor subject – but, of course, the only way that will only happen is if our little tribes start slaughtering each other again; the Hague is close by, but you know, they won't always be hiring translators and, I don't know, experts in savage thinking and advocates for multiculturalism; I'm sorry, but it's all just the usual bullshit, Gospođa Spomenka said and buried her face in her hands; maybe one or two of them has a personal connection with these things, is the child of immigrants, or refugees like me, she said with a strange spark in the corner of her dark eye, so they quickly latch on to me, but I don't make any excuses for them; I always tell them, literature is no cure for homesickness – that's what I talk to them about, that's what I've been trying to tell them for almost twenty years, Gospođa Spomenka said as somebody knocked on the tall double doors, grey from smoke, in this office in a side corridor, with a blocked and limited view of a busy street; so who's interrupting me now? Gospođa Spomenka said; Pavel, go open the door, she said; they're probably upset about the smoke again, although nobody here ever knocks, Gospođa Spomenka said. Pavel lowered his cigarette, drowned it in the coffee cup, and went to the door; just a moment, he said amiably and opened the door into the corridor, which was completely empty, quiet; it must have been a mistake, Pavel said; well you see, Gospođa Spomenka said, I thought so; she sighed and shifted in her chair, making herself more comfortable; Kiš, Crnjanski, Andrić, she said sharply, thinking for a moment as if searching for another name to add – now that is literature, but today? Give me just one name that means something today in that region we somehow still have in common; there aren't any, not since we tore our country apart and went off in different directions all over the world, like people without any sense of greatness or culture inside them; there is no one any more. I stood up and put out my cigarette on the coffee saucer; Pavel opened the high lancet window to let the smoky stale air out of the office in the old university. Outside, across the street, blocking the pallid sun, a tall rectangular silo rose into the late-afternoon sky; there were birds flying around it. That's Boekentoren, Pavel said, where the university library is; we should have a look, it's quite grand, it was designed by Henry van de Velde; yes, you see, while we and the Krauts were slaughtering each other in the forest, here they built libraries to the sky, Gospoda Spomenka said; it's beautiful, but it's too big and bright for me, too empty and cold; here again you see that difference I was trying to tell you about; we don't have this sort of mentality. The soft, concrete-grey shadow of the library tower settled for a moment over the office, and the blue cigarette smoke weaving slowly above our heads now suddenly turned darker. The shimmering dust, falling slowly, spinning and, with every emphasized word, sailing up again to the high ceiling, from the yellowed scribbled papers, the photocopies and fat binders, now, with the next unspoken word, alighted on the illegible dog-eared notes pasted to the walls. The past and the darkness were settling on the Faculty of Arts and Philosophy with the silence, with an unutterable question they were slowly sifting down, blanketing the office at the end of the corridor, and the dust, without shine, knitted itself into thick clumps, which hung off the yellowed edges of crumpled flyers and posters from conferences and symposia long past; we sat there without speaking, surrounded by ash-coloured walls and in the shadow of the tall concrete silo full of books, which was blocking the bashful sun; for a long time we sat, and even after we stood up, when we were saying our goodbyes, as our cigarettes glowed dimly between our fingers and somewhere outside a wind started blowing upriver so that the sky was clear and the air was moving above the earth, we were, each within ourselves, weighing and sorting – although amazingly we still understood each other – were turning in our hands something that had been stored away completely and lost, each of us, our memories, fear and anger. Dust was falling on to dust. Here, take it; call me when you come to Antwerp; that's where I live, Gospođa Spomenka said as she offered me her card; come for a visit, I'll show you the city. My Sarajevo simply abandoned me, but Antwerp took me in; this is my city now and I couldn't live anywhere else, Gospođa Spomenka said and slowly, through smoke and ash, left the office. The professor's voice was soon spreading through the corridors of the venerable university, in a language that perhaps only Pavel and I, leaving the foyer, and a very few students could understand, saying that somewhere there was once a land with a great literature, where charismatic writers had lived, but now those cities are no more and only ashes and unjust borders remain to tell of them, and their great writers have all died, are scattered in foreign languages or have drowned in minor-language translations, in a flood of mediocrity, which we once so despised, Gospođa Spomenka said – even long after the smell of cigarette smoke had melted away, seeping into the faded plaster of the venerable European university.

Above the grey of the sky and this late-afternoon earth there shone a buttery light with no sharp shadows or distracting reflections; the wind rippled and rocked the many-branched, strong-walled network of arteries through which the slowed-down water slowly moved, carrying on its surface a somewhat darkened, wavy image of the city in displaced perspective; what a lovely light, I thought, as if designed for an amateur travel photographer. Graceful in colour and harmonious in architecture, the view of the medieval city was simply offering itself, opening itself to the pampered eye, with its many shapely stone bridges – one of which I was now standing in the middle of, admiring the slender church belfries with their golden clocks, the stone defence towers and walls, which rose above the high pointed roofs and bright yellow, white and ochre-brown façades, accented by dark beams, on the former guild houses of merchants, lawyers and artisans, which playfully and yet with a certain staid arrogance took their privileged place in the scrupulously restored and finished crown of buildings on the embankment – a favourite motif of the old Flemish masters of landscape and genre painting. But a gust of wind, slightly colder and sharper, strengthened, hastened and honed by contact with the walled canals and narrow, tight passages in the crooked side streets, and sharpened further as it travelled beneath the river's many low bridges, a gust that had suddenly pulled upriver just as a light cloud covered the meagre sun, now as the next bell chimed in I don't know which little tower, was erasing the mirage of the city on the river's murky surface, and the reflection, the image, overexposed in the soft, veiled light of eternity, which is more real than the restored city outline, went dark. There's nothing left, nothing at all, everything is gone, it suddenly occurred to me; I was standing in the middle of the low, paved bridge, which curved across the river-canal in an arc, when suddenly from somewhere, as I was searching my pockets for my camera, I heard the sharp, disillusioned and emotion-laden words of Gospoda Spomenka: these days our so-called writers travel the whole wide world with their unpublished manuscripts, Gospoda Spomenka had told her students, and it was still echoing faintly somewhere, like a threat or evil destiny – and all these pseudo-writers are fervently searching for innocent ears that, at least superficially, can understand our many small languages, so they can share with foreigners their sadness and yearning, or whatever it was that my colleagues in Slovene studies used to say, Gospoda Spomenka said, which nobody can understand, but the truth is that nobody gives a damn any more about our eternal little Balkan wars, our Central European melancholy and nostalgia; you, and my beautiful daughter, too, you are all growing up today in a different world, so anything I talk about in my lectures, take it purely as a curiosity, something that, while possibly very interesting and attractive, is, of course, entirely foreign to you, and never fully accessible, like a beautiful poem by our great poet that you will never understand – the words maybe, but never the meaning; and, of course, the thing that interests you the most, well, I'll tell you: you can't make a living from it. I had lost my desire to take pictures. Pavel waved to me from the embankment and politely tapped his forefinger on his watch; I understood; we have to hurry, the students are waiting for me, he said as we quickly made our way to St Bavo's Cathedral, where we parted. Pavel stepped into a quiet, fast tram that soon left for the university; I lit a cigarette and looked at the clock; I was too early, I still had some time to myself, I thought, and put out the cigarette. I went up the low, long stone steps to the doors and looked back at the square in front of the cathedral; only a few people, wrapped in coats and thoughts, were hurrying across; in the distance you could hear the bell of a departing tram; a waiter in a white shirt and black apron came out of a nearby bistro carrying a tray with a glass of beer, a passer-by was photographing two female tourists in short sleeves, at their request, in front of the cathedral, and over the head of the saint with a golden thorny crown who stood in the middle of the square on a stone plinth with a downcast, quiet and distant gaze, and between the white clouds that floated above the city, the blue sky cleared. I entered the cathedral.

I remember we took a shortcut through the gorge to get back to the lake; Jane showed me that way, Gjini said, since people hardly ever went down there; now it looks like nobody takes it any more, it's all overgrown, but it wasn't so long ago that Jane and I would go for walks here. Just the grave, that old cross – it always seems the same to me, Gjini said as, sweating and panting, we strode down the little lakeside path towards the manor, which, all aglow, was veiled by the tree-lined path; only its turrets rose above the dark treetops; that's where you would have the finest view of the lake and even far beyond, I remember thinking. Beneath the thin mists that were floating on the water, there were little waves, long and shining, which rolled across the lake and made a burbling sound all their own; later – now, when Gjini and I had met again – I said that even today I would be able to tell them apart from all the other waves I had ever heard in my life, by their sound alone, that burbling, which was as though somebody on the opposite side had without hesitation dived into the cold lake and with strong, determined strokes was deftly, but softly and stealthily, swimming across, over to here, to the foot of the manor, where the waves became quiet and still and vanished into the sand; I said I would recognize those waves even if I never saw them again. Interesting, Gjini said when we had gone from the lake up to the spacious terrace in front of the manor's entrance; that's interesting; Jane, too, told me she often heard voices in the waves; she said that usually when she spent the night here and evening was coming on, when the last tourists and the day staff had left and the doors were shut to strangers, and only the Benedictine sisters remained, who had also withdrawn into their closed rooms, hidden from outsiders' eyes, in the upper wing of the manor, Gjini said and helpfully pointed his finger to an upper storey, so when Jane was suddenly left quite alone in this house, despite there being other people here, at the hour when the evening mist settled on the lake and a cool wind blew from the surrounding hills, with a patter of rain coming down like a dense and weightless silk curtain falling over the valley, Gjini said, that's when I would again hear that sound in the air, unmistakably, Jane said, Gjini said, as if in the lapping of the waves in the lake I was hearing the clip-clop of unshod horse hoofs, a shallow plash, a gallop across the surface. I don't know, said Jane. I don't know, Gjini said, this country is full of legends and fairy tales; these people are still surrounded by ghosts and fantastic creatures, as if the country was still waking up from sleep, from a midnight nightmare; despite having electricity, which, in fact, came relatively late here, people still stumble in the dark, still wander through the valleys and hide from the world, as if the real sun had never shone here. When I was a student I heard lots of incredible stories, legends and tales from the past, which amazingly even now hang over people's souls like a curse; despite their Christianity, which waged war against superstition, everything here is still full of magic and old-world beliefs. I used to talk to Jane about it, but she made fun of my scholarly observations and academic scepticism, and did so ever more openly and sincerely – the more she heard, and also the more she experienced here, repeatedly, as if time and again she, too, was slipping into some earlier sleep, the more she herself believed again. Your true home is where you believe the fairy tales, Jane said.

It was only here, when I was closer to the landscape again, and immersed myself in the shadows of my family's past, and at the same time opened up to the light I had discovered inside myself – it was only here that I realized I really could start taking photographs, Jane said; if I'm not mistaken, that was on her second visit, Gjini said, the first time we spent the night outside. That was when she started bringing her photo equipment with her on our trips, along with the obligatory notebooks and journals in which she was always making notes about everything. It wasn't long after the beginning of the autumn term; I had just returned to Galway after a short trip home, which I didn't want to tell her about yet, when she surprised me with her visit; she found me, even though we hadn't been in touch for a while; also, I was no longer running the stand at the bus station, where normally I had spent all my mornings before; in fact, I lost the sandwich job when I told my boss I was going home for a few weeks. So now there was nobody selling fresh sandwiches at the station because my boss couldn't find anyone willing to run the business, to get up early, be friendly and maintain good relations with the regular customers, make sure everything was clean, keep things tidy and at the same time behave properly – in other words, to work for not a lot of money; well, you know, I always got something on the side, some modest tips, which, by the way, is really unusual, people don't do that here, so I had to be especially witty and accommodating, and always give them something extra, a kind word or smile, since I knew I wasn't just selling people a sandwich, which the bus riders could have bought somewhere else, but everybody liked coming back to me and even paid a little more; that's important, I tell you, Gjini said; that's the way it is in any business – people have to like you, they have to know you. Everybody at the station knew me, travellers from near and far, on both the early-morning and lunchtime routes; they knew where to find me, Gjini said; I found out later that in the end my boss tried doing the work at the station himself, but he gave up after a few weeks and went out of business, that's what my mate at the news-stand told me, the one I used to borrow newspapers from, Gjini said; I still drop by to see him once in a while, when I'm in the area; I'll look through a newspaper and have a coffee with him from the machine; you know, it's good to have somebody, to know somebody, he said. He's the one who told me Jane had come back and was looking for me in the city, he said, that she still came there every morning, that even before he'd finished arranging the outside racks she'd buy a coffee in a plastic cup from the machine and leaf through the newspapers; he said he had the feeling that the only reason she came to the news-stand was to ask about me, if maybe I had come back or had stopped by, if he had heard anything from me or seen anything, if I had maybe come to the city by bus from somewhere, and then she would walk to one of the stops and smoke outside until the bus she was waiting for arrived to take her out of the city; of course, my mate couldn't tell her anything specific; all he could say was, I miss him, too, that Albanian's a good bloke, and he did better business than me, Jane told me later, when we finally found each other again. But Jane seems different to me now, like she's found something, my mate at the bus station news-stand told me. I know that feeling; I've been here too long not to know how to size people up; I see them coming and going, see them waiting, some patiently, others nervously, anxiously; I see them, and mainly it's the same people who've been coming through here for years and years; some of them I even recognize from when they were young, when they came here every day on the school bus, and later they came back as university students, and some of them left from here to go abroad for a long time, or even for ever; that's how it is: they go from the local bus station to Shannon, then on to a plane and far off into the sky, my mate from the news-stand said, but me, I'm always here; every day the daily news comes to me from all over the world; people arrive and depart – so how could I not get better over time, and I mean years and decades, at sizing people up, seeing their hidden character? You know what they say, Gjini my friend: you really know a person when you see them at a bus station, when they're leaving or returning; they're never the same when they come back, even less so when they're leaving; you can always tell if a person is leaving someone behind, or if there's someone waiting for them, missing them, because you know, people here are made out of things like goodbyes – final, permanent, painful goodbyes. Famine, death, homesickness, it's left its mark on us, this goddamn emigration – there are more of us living somewhere else than here at home, my mate said; no offence, but that's how I see it; there's something of that in you, too; maybe that's why we get along so well, and understand each other even better than we think we do, my mate told me, Gjini said. Yes, I thought Jane seemed different, as if she had finally found and read that line, that quote, that word which suddenly transformed her, which for a long time she had been looking for in archives, in dusty, yellow newspapers and thick books, something that for her was new, even if it had been buried in the earth or lost at sea for many years; yes, that's how she seemed to me those mornings when she came by herself to the station and you weren't here any more. It's obvious Jane misses you very much, and I think she has something she wants to tell you, Gjini; you need to get in touch with her, my mate said. Patrick is his name; he's put on some weight these past few years, and he's a little older, but he's had some luck in his life – like that news-stand at the bus station; it's a good business; people will always be travelling and reading, and eating sandwiches, too – these things go together; I expect they got that from the English, Gjini said when we met again in Ghent. A few days, maybe a week at most, before my arrival here, we had exchanged a few emails, after being long out of touch. I wrote him that I was about to leave on my trip and that other than a few obligations I would again have some valuable time for writing and unhurried travel around the country; I'm attaching the picture I took of you, you'll know where it was, I added. Gjini wrote back at once; he reported in full detail that after a long and intensive search he had found a new part-time job at the City Council in the city's Culture and Education Committee; finding work is getting harder and harder, he wrote and at the end added that he, too, would be glad if he could take a few days off work and join me, especially, he wrote, because I'd like to tell you about what I've been working on for a while now; I'm writing an article for *The Galway*

Advertiser; not long ago I met with the newspaper's editor and gave him a thorough account of my background; I proposed that he take me on as a freelance contributor; I offered to compile and edit, on a weekly or monthly basis, a page devoted to poetry; mainly I'd be publishing literary texts by writers from Connemara, and later maybe other writers, too. People here are so incompetent, he wrote; there's so much poetry being written but nobody responds to it – I'm going to see if I can change that, he wrote. But to start with, I'm putting together a large feature on Kylemore Abbey; I wrote about it when I was a student, you know, he told me, but now he had discovered an entirely new angle. I'm finding it harder to write, and now that it's all become, in a way, personal, everything's different. I, too, have been thinking about and planning a trip to Belgium for some time; there are a few places I need to visit, places Jane told me about, of course, Gjini wrote in his last email before I left. I'll definitely have more to tell you when we meet; friendly regards and hope to see you soon. Gjini. P.S. thanks for the picture; I'm sending you a photo from your literary evening in Galway; I found it on my phone; greetings to Suzana, Boris and Gašper. After this message he didn't write to me again before I left, so I didn't know what he had decided.

I didn't believe Jane and I would ever see each other again, not at that time; I was filled with doubt and worry, and at first, for a moment, I was hesitating, wondering if I'd be able to manage it all; I still had a few things overdue that I had to finish or pass at college before I could register for the final year, and I was running out of time; I had no money left – I had used it for my trip to Albania and left the remainder of my savings with my family at home; you know how it is, Gjini said, there's always somebody who depends on you. She did seem different to me, changed, and not only in appearance, although her hair was longer, I thought and right away tried to compose myself so she wouldn't catch me out, so I didn't hurt her feelings; it's the sugar, she said, as if reading my thoughts; they discovered I have diabetes, and the doctor put me on insulin; don't worry, it runs in the family, I've got it under control, Jane said, Gjini said; I was only trying to hide my surprise, since it had been a few long and turbulent months, almost since the spring – there was a whole summer between us since we'd said goodbye – and I must have looked different in her eyes, too, since I was still contorted and crumpled from the narrow bed in my former

homeland, but, I'll say it again, at the time I still wasn't able to tell her, Gjini said; I myself only learned the happy news two months later, that I was expecting a child, he said; I was going to have to find a way to bring them here soon, but I still didn't know how – despite everything, I was just an immigrant, but even so; I feel like I'm ready to do photography now, but I think it might be too late for me, Jane said. We were sitting by the fire. We were hiding from the rain and the wind, which wailed across the empty landscape; every so often bolts of lightning would flash high over the black sky, without any thunder; the storm was raging somewhere far away over the sea, threatening the ships, but even so, we were as wet as if we had fallen in the ocean. We were lucky, Gjini said; by mere chance, in total darkness, we had stumbled on a shepherd's shelter, after really and truly getting lost, which we at least admitted to ourselves, since we had stayed too long in the remote interior, after turning back in the early afternoon from the sea, which had been calm, still and dark. Across its vast expanses shining in the sun, which had darted out from behind the shapeless clouds, the sea was flashing with the gleam of old burnished silver. We were strolling along, or rather, walking at a quick pace, on a sandy and probably long-neglected path on the edge (for me, too close to the edge) of the overhanging cliffs; far below, where I had no desire to look, I heard only the insolent birds and the sound of the sea, Gjini said; the car was at least a couple miles downhill on a road next to the sea; stop here, we can leave the car here, Jane had said without warning. We were driving slowly along a narrow winding road, which had become suddenly wider when we left Roundstone, without having stopped there, although that had been her initial desire, to stop in this small fishing village, have a glass of beer on the pier by the boats and go for a walk in the village and surrounding area, where the painter Jack Butler Yeats had once rambled in search of views to inspire him; I love his muted, cloudy colours and the vehemence in his brushstroke – have you studied him yet at the college? Jane had asked; but when we had come quite close to the sea – the road here runs right by the shoreline – she suddenly said, no, let's go somewhere higher up, I'd like some air, I need a view. I drove slowly along the little road that went between, on one side, the boats in the shallow dock and, on the other, the pubs in front of which men were sitting in short sleeves with woollen caps on their heads. It was somewhere here that I spent the night, in the attic of one of these pubs, the last time I was walking here, Jane said; I got caught in a downpour so I couldn't leave; it was impossible to go any further; the rain was coming down hard, making such a noise on the roof that it calmed and somehow softened the heavy voices from the pub below; I was cold and succumbing to loneliness, to an anxiety that for several years had lain dormant inside me, although I knew from experience that it could wake up at any time from its half-slumber, Jane said, but ever since I started coming here, to these shores, and if I think about it, ever since I have been travelling around Europe, everything within me has somehow got easier, which is why I come here more and more often and stay longer each time, she said; that unhoped-for invitation I received, and it will soon be four years now, somehow set me free, she said; it arrived like a message in a bottle that had been tossed long ago into the sea. I was breathing as if trapped below decks on a rickety boat far out on the waves; with a damp blanket wrapped around me, I stood on a chair and on tiptoes looked out through the skylight at the sea; the window was flooded on the outside, so all I could see were dense zigzags of rain on the angled glass; I will have to open it, I thought as I stood helpless beneath the ceiling on the chair, peering into the shimmer of the water; for a moment, I thought I saw something flashing, a whiteness in the saturated clouds; I need to get out – if I don't, I'll suffocate. Banging on the window sash with both my hands, I pushed it open; I don't remember if I broke it, but I felt a little better when, looking through the narrow crack of the partly opened frame, between the raised window and the drenched roof, I could again see far into distance. On the wavy, windy brownish water, not far from the moorings beside the road we're driving on right now, Jane said, or maybe by then I had lost all sense of depth and perspective, obliterated by the low, motionless, sepia-toned sky – even now I see the perfectly drawn parallels, from sky to earth, down which the rain fell in long, solid lines, Jane said; I soon calmed down, and only then could I see the slow, listing single-masted wooden boat, which had caught the wind in its white sail. It wasn't making for the shore, for shelter, but instead, it sailed along the shoreline – in the same direction we're going, Jane said. It was only later, after I had been gazing a long time into the emptiness, moderating my breathing with deep breaths that barely kept pace with the rhythm of the waves, she said, and by then the sailboat was far beyond the bay, had maybe arrived at its destination, completed its journey – that's when it dawned on me that there had been mourners on the deck – hunched over, silent, in wet black coats, they were crowded around a coffin, which later they must have carried from the boat and set down on rocks surrounded by soggy and eternally green grass; then, lifting it in a single motion, they would have placed it on their drooping shoulders and with short, slow steps carried it along a winding sandy lane to a churchyard strewn with old, leaning crosses, Jane said; that's how I walked with them in my thoughts even later – many times, she said; in fact, whenever it rains on the sea I think of that mournful journey. Eventually, when the rain let up, the funeral procession would have taken the same well-trodden path back down to the sea, they would have untied the bowline and sat down again in the old boat with bottles of whisky in their hands. They're still sailing on the sea, Jane said; even today they're sailing on the sea. I said nothing; I didn't feel like talking; I felt the same way I had felt almost a year earlier, at the beginning, when I was still really just the driver, and in a way I liked that; it suited me to have somebody attentive, who was ready to listen to my boring lectures about ruins, emigration, famine, the damned English and dry academic interpretations of fairy tales, although I soon learned that Jane knew a great deal more than I did; she knew everything, in fact, but she also knew how to keep things to herself, I quickly realized, so I had only a rather definite sense of it, knew only that she carried something inside her that I would never hear or read about anywhere else. Tell me something about yourself, Jane said, I'd like to get to know you, Gjini;

I looked at her and said nothing, Gjini said. Let's go on foot from here, she said; the light is beautiful; I'd like to take a few pictures to remember it by. Although I kept driving on for a while, slowly, checking the slippery grey road that more or less abutted the shallow sea from which dark rocks were protruding, while on the other side, on the right, high, golden-brown grass was growing from a bank of sand the wind must have deposited – where the car could easily have got stuck – so although I drove on as if looking for a suitable place to park, in fact, to be honest, I wasn't very keen on a long walk, which I knew from experience would stretch into the evening or the night, and I didn't know what Jane was really up to; from the moment we met the day before, I had found her so terribly different, in some indescribable but palpable way; she seemed to be looking at me from a distance, but trustingly, and I kept trying to find the right words to approach her, to address her, although now I know it had nothing to do with my merely superficial knowledge of a language that was foreign to me – it was, you could say, something beyond language; I know that now, Gjini said. Jane had sought me out because she wanted to have somebody to walk with in silence, because she had found something that gave her life meaning and wanted to share it, but I didn't know that then, when I was trying to make excuses, saying I couldn't just leave the car here alone; it would be better if we drove further on to admire the panoramic view, I told Jane and gently pressed down on the accelerator to go a little higher above the sea, where there was a beautiful view of the rolling landscape, which by now was completely green; behind a low stone wall, on a ridge where the land dropped into the sea, was a small cemetery with tilted crosses; stop the car, you can let me off here, I'll go on by myself, Jane said, quite calmly; wait for me in Ballyconneely; I'll see you there. I turned on to a soft patch of grass and stopped the car; our eyes met and we understood each other perfectly. Jane got out and walked away without closing the door, almost impatiently, which I had never seen in her before, but rather the opposite, I'd say: she had always known how to wait; patience and perseverance were qualities she nurtured in herself; I saw her leave the road and walk to the cemetery. She didn't look back; I waited by the car, just as I had done the first time I took her on one of these trips and really was just the driver. Soon, in the distance, on the soft, grassy overhang, I saw her dark shape moving among the old stone crosses, across which the soft shadows of the clouds were drifting; I don't remember if she called to me or maybe just waved; I smiled back at her, although she was too far away to see. Then she disappeared behind the low stone markers as if she had seen or found something. It was a while before she came back; I was still politely waiting for her, leaning against the car, even if in the meantime nothing anywhere had altered its appearance or even moved; it's as though she stepped out of a photograph, I thought; I see her again as she was before, months ago, when we last saw each other – unchanged, lively and bright. I left the camera in the car, Jane said and turned away to face the sea; it's strange, but I had the feeling I had never gone away, like I had never left this place. We shouldered our light backpacks, which held our lunch and, mainly, her camera equipment – that was something new for me – and, without any chart or map, set off on what we imagined would be a circular route; I haven't forgotten – don't worry, we won't be late – I remember this way, I've walked here before, Jane said, and we continued on foot, as she had wanted. After a long and gentle incline that made a sharp bend, which, in our initial enthusiasm, we covered quickly and mostly in silence, the road descended gradually to the shore; I had been walking in front of her a while, gazing at the open landscape, which was silent and completely empty, but now, when the only thing I still heard behind my sweat-drenched back, bent beneath its burden, was her breathing, as if she was whispering into the wind or mimicking the waves, something invisible to the eye and far from here, but already announcing itself, this thing we could not yet tell each other – so now, when all I could still hear were my own footsteps, I had the sudden feeling of being left alone in the world; at that moment, when all I could see was the sun shining on the water in long diaphanous ribbons, her whisper, her gentle, restrained breathing, slipped past me; I felt it distinctly graze my shoulder and recede into the distance, ever more softly; I saw the tracks in the lightly pressed grass, in the fine sand on the shore and then in the slight rippling of the water's surface; she is leaving, I thought; she is running back to the sun.

It's splendid; I had no idea it would be so big, and it's beautiful, exactly the way Jane described it to me, Gjini said. He was talking in a loud voice, too loud for the serious, somewhat bored and weary attendant who was standing behind a high, black counter relieving visitors, who had no chance to protest, of their handbags, backpacks and cameras and offering them in exchange devices with audio guides and headphones. At his solemn caution to respect the silence, and after receiving many dark and disdainful looks from the other visitors the instant the man issued his warning, Gjini, with a smile, removed his headphones so as not to be so disturbingly loud; do you remember, he said, the miniature copy we saw in Kylemore Abbey? The Benedictine sisters brought it over from the convent in Ypres, which had been destroyed, he said;

Jane adored it; she said we'd have to come here one day and see the original together; she had been here at least twice, if I'm not mistaken, Gjini said. He was standing behind my back, at my left shoulder, speaking in a hushed voice. He had surprised me with his sudden arrival; the newspaper sent me to take pictures for the article, and the editor agreed to it, Gjini told me later; I had entered the side chapel of St Bavo's Cathedral only some ten minutes before. Without a word, the attendant had merely pointed a finger at my bag, taken it and pushed headphones into my hands; I thanked him and left them on the counter. The high, narrow semicircular space was suffused with a bluish light, muted and veiled, coming from the reflector lamp that dimly and without reflection illuminated a tall Plexiglas partition, behind which the polyptych *The Lamb of God* stood open on a tall wooden base. In the warm, dry air you could hear an unintelligible chatter, a blend of languages escaping from under the headphones as visitors kept putting them on and taking them off again. I stepped closer to the Plexiglas and gazed at the magnificent painting. I'll wait for you outside, Gjini said, covering his ears with the headphones. I saw him weave carefully through the visitors engrossed in the painting and vanish into the unlit narrow passage that circled behind the protected work, which I myself later entered in order to view the polyptych from the back, to admire as well the unfolded panels painted with saints, who were only accessible from the front when the composition was closed.

I spent a few minutes in front of the new Town Hall, Gjini said when we met again outside, in front of the cathedral; of course, I'm mainly attracted to the medieval one, which stands in respectful defiance behind the new building, where it's been for nearly five hundred years, but Jane told me she was unusually drawn to the construction and modern design of the contemporary Town Hall, which on her last visit here they were still putting the finishing touches to; she said it made an extraordinary impression on her, especially because of its lightness, its physicality and unusual emptiness, which captivated her when she stood beneath the high roof, which is supported only by unfinished concrete pillars without any surrounding walls – the administrative offices, city services and public areas are all underground, hidden beneath a little green lawn, she told me excitedly – so all the space beneath the roof turns into one expansive window, Jane said; I looked out at the square, she said, which was lined with medieval belfries and baroque buildings – the open form has thus appropriated the quaint façades around it and, in a sense, the entire city, the entire world and the sky, too, its blueness, fog and rain; it has made them all its own, Jane said, Gjini said to me; I had the impression that the great volume of the space, which is bounded above, merely sketched out, as it were, by a roof construction of wooden beams, with the void trapped beneath a lightweight, simple but at the same time imposing cover that makes the interior seem unconfined – that it was literally boundless – here, of course, Jane had intuited the architect's idea, which perhaps is telling visitors about the openness, accessibility and temporary nature of the earthly institutions symbolized by the architecture, Gjini said; I might agree with her view, but my speciality, and my personal affinity, too, is mainly historical things, that is to say, everything that speaks of permanence, immutability, maybe even eternity, which is why I love historical styles, and ruins, too, the remnants, if you will; I don't know, I told Jane, how can empty space speak about eternity? What will remain of it in the future? Gjini said.

We quickly left St Bavo's Square, above which dark grey clouds were now hanging; Gjini glanced up at them; I recognize this weather: it's

just like ours, it's going to start pouring soon – the Gulf Stream brings the rain from the sea, Gjini said and, opening the black leather men's handbag that was always hanging from his wrist, he pulled out a long grey poncho and slipped it over his head; then we went down to the canals of the Leie River, which moved lazily along beneath the arches of the low bridges, but soon, at the city's edge, it would converge with the Scheldt and then flow in a broad stream across Flanders to Antwerp – which I would be visiting in the coming days – and at the wide mouth pour into the sea, from which, indeed, a slow rain was soon to arrive above our heads. It fell perpendicularly on the streets and the river, parallel to the belfries, the city walls and the library in the tower, which I told Gjini about on the way to Sint-Pieters train station, where we would have to say goodbye temporarily. It was finished only a few months before the First World War, Gjini said – we were standing beneath the brick clock tower in front of the station – they had modernized and expanded it as an architectural contribution to the 1913 World's Fair, which was held in Ghent – what irony! – as I said, not long after the close of the exhibition, just a few months later to be exact, the most brutal and tragic war the world had ever seen began not far from here, as if the old gang from the fair had started brawling and slaughtering each other, Gjini said and pulled the wet, long, grey poncho over his head and shook it against the ground. Maybe the worst of it was right there in Ypres, which was razed to the

ground, and in the surrounding area, where you can still see miles of well-preserved trenches; this is where the Germans first used nerve gas – Yperite it's called; it's horrible – I had never heard of anything like it, Jane said to me, Gjini said. I rented a bike and spent the whole day riding across the endless plain of Flanders – green and grassy and windy – to breathe, she said; I went to all the trenches, as if I would find the answer there, Jane said; something was speaking to me, whispering from the land, although I had never imagined – but now I know – that this, too, somewhere here on this plain, could be my home. This gorgeous landscape stained with the blood of the innocent – it's horrible, Jane said, and virtually all of Europe was

dying here, and with it the entire familiar world; mine, too, the one I wanted to escape from, Gjini said, down there in the Balkans, where you and I were born, that's where it all started. He was silent. I'm going back to Brussels, I said; I still have a few obligations there and I'd like to take some short trips, I said, like I wrote to you. The wind was blowing the rain towards the station entrance; there were only a few travellers with bags going in and coming out; the trains were departing and arriving almost soundlessly; we retreated a few steps, to beneath a modern, semicircular glass canopy, designed in imitation of Art Nouveau with stylized floral wreaths; I lit a cigarette; Gjini had finished storing his poncho in the handbag and pulled out a train ticket; I sensed that he was focused on his trip, or maybe something else was growing inside him – ivy, I thought, encircling him, spreading over him – he was excited and distant, as if he had forgotten for a moment that he wasn't waiting outside by himself. She said she rode the bike all the way to the coast, twenty-five miles, to Koksijde, Gjini said; I wanted to touch the North Sea, she said, to cool off, drown, disappear even, Jane said; I left the bike in the high dunes the moment I saw the sea in the distance, the moment I heard the waves, and ran through the tall, dry grass to the wide and sandy shore, which went on for miles, she said; it was a lonely place, a terrible wind was blowing, the sea was grey, low, with even waves; I sensed it coming slowly towards me, I knew the tide was coming in. I hid in the dunes, lay in the sparse clumps of dry grass and curled into a ball, she said. All was quiet again; I am not here, I have not been born yet, I thought, Jane said. I'm not sure but it was as if the wind carried it in from the sea; it hovered in the silence, somewhere deep inside me, not a song, but the singing of angels; the dead were still singing, Jane said, Gjini said; I was hearing again the exalted, hope-filled singing of the boys, still almost children, who were lying in the cold, muddy trenches, Jane said; it was Christmas Eve in the year 1914, the first year of the terrible war was passing – in the autumn, the boys still trusted their absent emperors, kings and generals, who told them they would be home by Christmas, but now, as the hour was approaching midnight, they knew they would lie here for ever, and maybe only the song would remain, carried by the wind over the scorched grass, Jane said, Gjini said; I had read about it at the military museum – the *Weihnachtsfrieden*, the Germans called it, she said, and now, as I lay there in the dunes utterly alone, I again heard them singing, rising out of the trenches as if from graves, everyone laying down their arms, Germans and English, each on their own side of the front line, singing a Christmas carol into the wind, into the night – which for many of them would never end, Jane said, Gjini said.

I'm in a hurry, Gjini said; I want to catch the first train, he said and stepped quickly through the wide doors into the station concourse; I put out my cigarette and followed him in; I saw him running through the corridor and looked at the departures board, where the information had just been updated; Ypres, seven minutes, I read. I looked over to where Gjini had disappeared; an illuminated sign was hanging above the corridor, and among the other symbols on it there was one with a suitcase and key; he's gone to get his luggage, I thought; I'll wait here, he'll have to come back this way. Exactly three minutes passed before he returned through the long corridor to the concourse, where I was waiting for him anxiously; angry and out of breath, he pulled a wheeled suitcase behind him; they don't understand a thing, he said, not a thing; I told them I was running late but – forget it, Gjini said; I'll call you, he said and went straight down the stairs into the deep, long tunnel to the platforms; I was only able to take a few steps after him, wanting to help him with his luggage, before he disappeared; I looked at the board – Ypres, two minutes – he'll make it, or maybe not, I thought. Perhaps there would still be time for us to sit in peace and have a glass of pale lager; there were lots of trains leaving in our directions; the next one is in forty minutes, I thought, but probably Gjini really was in a hurry, although he had not had time to tell me why. Two minutes passed, and only one person emerged from the tunnel and came up the steep, wide stairs – a new arrival, holding a light briefcase, newspaper and umbrella. He stopped in the middle of the concourse and looked around as if lost; just moments before I had watched him walk past me, confident and sure of himself, as if I didn't exist, but now I thought he looked lost, as if he was missing his eyeglasses. But there was no Gjini coming out of the tunnel. I turned and looked at the board: Bruxelles/Brussel, twenty minutes – and went out to the street. I lit a cigarette; the rain had stopped.

Across the great, black dome of the sky, which at its most distant hazy edges descended over a rolling nocturnal landscape, the sparks of myriad stars were flickering; I can't remember the last time I saw them, it occurred to me; somewhere far below, in the darkness, somewhere I couldn't see, in the quiet after the storm, I heard the sound of flowing water. That's what I was looking for: drinkable water; bucket in hand, I walked across the slippery grass and went down into a hollow through boggy ground. Just a few resolute steps after leaving our hideout above, I was overcome by a strange and powerful feeling that this was my home, as if I was a child again, far away somewhere in a hidden, wordless godforsaken place, where I knew the way and could name things even in the middle of the night. Although I suspected that I might have gone a bit off course, for no good reason but the inexplicable joy I felt at the sense of freedom washing over me I knew I was safe here. The house, the abandoned dwelling beneath the top of a gentle slope with the stars shining above it, where Jane and I had sought shelter, was soon far behind me, far from where I now stopped to calm my heartbeat and temper my breathing, which was drowning out all external sound so that the only thing I heard was the euphoric echo of my inner self; I knew I was very close to the water, and after just a few minutes' walk, on the edge of a peat bog where the ground again rose steeply into the next gentle slope, which was shining with a moist silver glow, I saw the rushing stream, but at that very instant I became distracted by a quite different sound; I took a moment to think; although Jane had kindly and graciously said that we could spend the night here, I was against it; I still wanted to get back to the city; I said I would find a road and walk to the car, which couldn't be far away, I told Jane; maybe now that the storm has passed, there will be somebody driving in that direction and I'll get them to stop, I said; Gjini, Jane said, we can spend a peaceful night here; take the bucket and go find a stream for water, so we can wash; I'll start a fire and we can dry off first, and I'll boil water for tea, she said and pushed the bucket into my hands, and in the morning we'll drive on to Kylemore Abbey, she said when I was already standing on the stone threshold; I think there's something I should finally tell you, Jane said – words that are still with me, that won't let me go. I heard a car, and then saw its headlights, which in slow twists and turns lit up the night and the surrounding emptiness. I ran across the soggy, muddy ground, which was sinking beneath my feet; I slipped and fell on my knees and picked myself up again, the bucket banging against my legs, but I didn't take my eyes off the car, which in the distance was driving at a steady speed through the darkness. I was shouting, was maybe even waving the bucket as I stumbled along; I was sure no other car would pass by that night; not a living soul lived anywhere around here any more; the houses had been empty for decades, some for a century, or were completely abandoned; only on occasion did people come here from the city, to spend the weekend maybe, or the owners of the large flocks of sheep that grazed freely on the wide meadows might spend the night in one of the houses; but I had suspected at once what I only later learned for a fact, namely, that Jane knew where we would get lost and where we could find safe shelter, and I was certain she knew whose house it was where she now, surely, was waiting anxiously for me to return. I crossed the cold, rushing stream, went right through the middle of it, sinking almost to my waist when I stepped into the water, and then, as fast as I could, I crawled on my knees up the opposite bank, and soon came to the road. I stood directly in front of the headlights – dripping and muddy, with a bucket in my hand. I intercepted the car at the last possible moment, before it had escaped me for ever and melted into the night; the headlights blinded me, so

I saw neither the car nor the driver. A pleasant voice asked if I needed assistance, and, when the door opened, the first thing I heard was music from the radio, which echoed through the lonely, silent, seemingly deserted landscape; no thank you, I'm just having a walk, I said, as soon as I felt the bucket in my hand. I have to get back to Jane, and, in fact, I wanted to remain with her – that's what hit me, although not quite so clearly, Gjini said; I still wasn't sure, but at that moment I decided without hesitation to stay with her, even if it meant . . . Gjini said and fell silent; the signal from the loudspeaker had again distracted him; it introduced a voice that provided the current arrival and departure information, and by now we recognized it unerringly, having been listening to it for nearly a full hour. We were sitting next to the big panoramic window in the station's café, watching the dense mesh of train tracks, electric wires and light signals, while in the background the voice from the PA system calmly announced the current train schedule in three languages. Gjini, sipping his second cup of black tea, flinched every time the signal came over the loudspeaker; I cannot miss the next train; I have to be in Ypres this afternoon, before it gets dark, he said and rose quickly from the table; I need to run, I'll be in touch; we will definitely see each other again in a few days; OK! I said with no chance to add anything else; I remained in my chair and followed him with my eyes as he went out behind me pulling the wheeled suitcase, which bumped against the crowded plastic chairs and lightweight tables; when he reached the bar he greeted the waiter, a black man, in a loud, friendly voice as if he had known him a long time; the man, surprised and smiling, watched him from behind a tall coffee-grinding machine, which was next to an open display case with *tramezzini*, baguettes and croissants; then Gjini slipped out of view, disappearing into the uniform, silent and fast-moving column of clerks, students, workers and day tourists rushing down the wide, steep staircase into the tunnel beneath the station, to the platforms, where every few minutes various compositions of express trains were filling and emptying; it was the afternoon rush and I knew I would no longer be able to escape the crowds, which would last far into the evening, so it would be best to leave as soon as possible if I didn't want to miss my next meeting in Brussels, where I was expected in the late afternoon; but his words were still pounding inside me, pouring down like the rain had poured that day when Gjini suddenly left me alone in the car in the middle of a deluge; I remembered it was on the way to Kylemore Abbey, on my first trip there, and he had gone off into doomsday on foot. I have no idea, I thought, how long I was sitting there frozen, in the front seat, staring with vacant eyes into the damp and steam that clouded all the windows. I had felt the cold and my anxiety as they slowly and relentlessly filled the car, but there was still no sign of Gjini; I tried to distract myself with the thought that maybe he just needed to relieve himself, really badly, even in such conditions, or maybe he had noticed something on the road that I couldn't see through the fog, which perhaps had been carried there by a torrential stream – rocks, a large tree branch, mud, a person who had got drunk and lost his way, who had collapsed in the trackless wasteland, someone who lost hope and lay down in the flooded road, who can say? – all this was going through my mind. I wanted to help him; I tugged at the door handle, but it didn't give; I looked beneath the steering wheel: he had taken the key with him, surely out of habit, without realizing it; I sighed: so I will just have to wait here patiently; I'm dry, locked in, I'm somewhere at least. I took my mobile out of my pocket and called Gjini; behind me on the back seat, his little black handbag started to ring. I began poking around, trying to distract my confused thoughts; I opened the compartment in front of me and shone my mobile into it; inside, neatly stacked, were notebooks bound in imitation leather and secured with elastic bands – three bigger black ones, a few in dark grey and one that was light blue; I recognized it at once. It was lying on the table in front of me now. Gjini had forgotten it when he left in a rush to catch his train. I discovered it when I picked up the newspaper that was lying on top. It's the same light-blue notebook from Gjini's car, I thought; I was absolutely certain. Quickly, I typed an SMS; he must already be on the train, I thought and wondered if I should run after him; there's no time to get it to him before he leaves: *You left your notebook on the table! My address: Hotel Astrid, rue du Cyprès, Brussels. See you.* It was still raining, just like the day I was locked in the car; nothing had changed. I stood up and moved away from the table; the café was now completely empty; all I heard was the rattle of porcelain coffee cups, which the waiter was buffing to a shine and stacking; I looked through the panoramic window at the train tracks; I suspected that the man behind the bar, too, was gazing into the distance – his image, hovering next to mine in the reflection on the glass, had become still; we were like a mirage, wandering souls trapped in the thoughts of those who move eternally from place to place; I stepped closer to the window, holding in my hands the light-blue notebook, again with an elastic band around it and bound in imitation leather. I peered into the trains that, below me, were leaving Sint-Pieters Station, hoping that in one of the accelerating express trains going past I would glimpse his misted image, similarly pressed to a window battered by rain – that we would exchange glances, would meet, fleetingly, one more time.

The late-afternoon sky was slowly, incrementally and without a trace melting away, although up here, at my line of vision, it was still possible to see blue, but below, on the horizon, which in the distance was joined to the metropolitan cityscape, above which rose only the tall spikes of the old tapering belfries, the tiny flashing lights of the telecommunication antennas and the big satellite dishes mounted on the roofs of the skyscrapers, the pre-evening shadow had fallen, and somewhere far in the background, where the apparent perimeter of the earth curved away – although anything within sight must have been within arm's reach, for I was standing on a hill, on Place Royale, around the corner from the Magritte Museum, which I had already been to, and from here, for the first time, I had the city in the palm of my hand, so to speak –on that invisible edge, then, as if high above the fathomless universe, which surrounded the city and from which the evening glow was shining, aeroplanes were lifting into the sky,

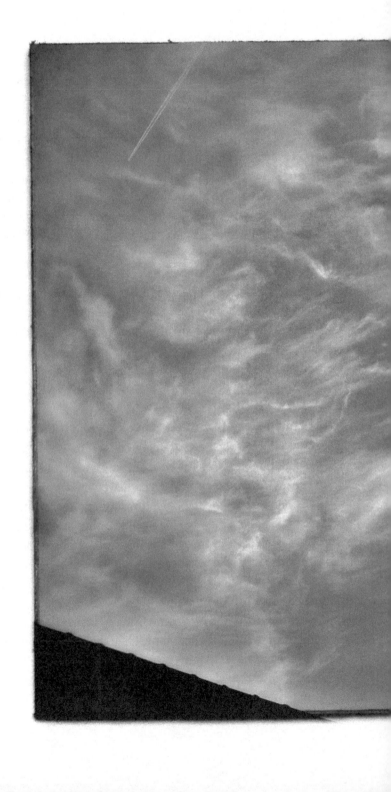

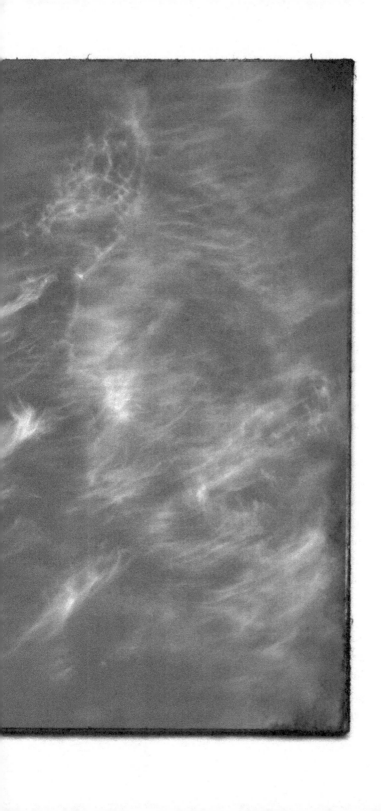

slowly and steeply, with a slight inclination of their bodies, going home, I thought, they're flying home, as I followed their short but bright trails of condensation, which instantly dispersed as the plane ascended into the great dome of the pastel-blue, fully translucent sky, on which lay big cumulus clouds, like dozens of enormous balloons floating above the world, balloons to which the hollow and nearly weightless ball of the earth is tied by thin cords; the flame in its core is dying out, I thought, and will soon be dark, we will grow cold and be hidden in infinity. I sat down on the wide white steps that made their way gently down Mont des Arts to the central railway station, where three days earlier I had been waiting for Pavel, and further on, to the historic core of the city, which in ever widening circles wrapped itself around Grand Place, the square I had passed through several times that day and which had made me feel anxious – each time, from whatever side I entered it, it had been full of tourists wearing hiking boots and long ponchos, their heads covered by hoods or wide-brimmed linen hats, with shopping bags, heavy cameras and plastic water bottles in their hands; as if time has stopped, the thought came to me, or maybe it simply wound itself back to the age of medieval pilgrimages, carnivals and feast-day processions; in the morning guided sightseeing tour we see the spirit of our lost piety, our quest for meaning, returning in perverted form, I thought; the long and lonely pilgrimages of the lowly, the hungry, the sick and the devout are now, it appears, replaced by popular, attractive and affordable tourist packages, which embody within us once more a sense of excitement, longing and mystery; for even in the safe and comfortable, quick journey of tourists with full bellies and no worries, who, having slowly grown tired and bored, little by little, with their companions, their shoes and the different languages, now traipse through the picturesque historic centres of cities, taking photo after photo, looking at little churches and big cathedrals, museums and restaurants – even here there is something beautiful and promised; here I seek peace – that's what I will write, I thought; time does not exist, it is merely a cognitive category by which we describe and partition unchangeable space, it occurred to

me; ever since the early morning I had been roaming and wandering aimlessly through the same, seemingly unchanged, narrow cobbled streets and open squares, as if I couldn't breathe, blending into the multitude of self-absorbed, agitated, hungry clerks, junior bank officers, estate agents, travel agents, business travellers and consultants, young male translators in running shoes and sports jackets and their female colleagues in bright-coloured blazers and light trench coats with elegant silk scarves draped around their shoulders, clutching protectively – both men and women alike, translators and simultaneous interpreters – their heavy, black computer bags, containing powerful laptops, tablets, external hard drives and designer USB sticks with downloaded pirate copies of vast multilingual dictionaries, compilations of legal, economic and social laws and regulations, either still in preparation or already in force in the EU and NATO. We're talking about a long, complex process of harmonization, in the political, economic and social arenas, certainly, but particularly in the legal sphere and, not least of all, in culture, Renata had said when we met in town the day before; she was a literary agent and occasional inter-preter for German and English at the European Parliament. She had been waiting for me patiently by the exit from the metro stop next to St Catherine's Church; I remember her standing in front of a burgundy-red circus trailer – I don't know how it got here, she told me later – and smoking a cigarette in the mild sunlight; when I walked by the spot this morning on the way from my hotel, the trailer was gone; they must have left in the night for somewhere far away, I thought. Renata had graciously offered to treat me to an early lunch at an Indian restaurant she liked, on a street just behind the building that housed the Brussels Bourse; it's early, I know, but at least it will be quiet enough for us to talk, she said. So how are you? Lots of work? I asked as we crossed a busy street when the light turned red; what we are trying to do, Renata said, and do in a way that is both consistent and based on the principle of equality, is to translate linguistic and conceptual diversity and difference into terminologically and culturally acceptable legislation, which will be accessible and, eventually, have legal force throughout the territory of the Union, and what's more, it needs to be understandable to all European citizens, she said; at least that's what they teach us, whatever it means in actual practice, she added and walked purposefully into the restaurant; I went in behind her; there was a folded card next to the candle on the table marking it as reserved; you think of everything, I said; well, you know I'm a practical woman – and you? Renata asked, how are you? OK? Are you writing? she asked, by which time an Indian man in a black suit had been standing for a while by our table, which had a view of the greying façade of the Bourse, now in shadow; we were his only guests, and he was content; I remember his patient, smiling face; *lady, please*, the waiter said; try the fish curry, Renata said, I recommend it, I always have it; OK, I said; *we'll both have the fish curry and two glasses of red wine*, Renata said; *merci, thank you*, the waiter said. I have my reading and discussion tonight at the House of Literature – Pavel is moderating, I said, thank you for your help; I know, I got the announcement, she said; unfortunately, I'm flying home this afternoon; I've already packed;

I feel like . . . she said, oh I don't know – we clinked our wine glasses – like nothing chimes any more here, not even the wine glasses, she said. After a few intense days of sitting all day in shaded, glass-walled corridors, waiting by the doors of different committees and sub-committees and commissions like some hothouse flower, I feel like something is draining out of me, unstoppably; my life is flourishing, I have a career, but even so, she said; look, we're drinking excellent wine, I'm here in my favourite restaurant – and believe me, you can't get curry like this in Ljubljana – but still I feel like I'm wilting, she said, burning out, and it doesn't take more than a few intense days in parliament, in the crowds, the confusion and stress, when there's always something that gets lost or needs to be adapted, with impossible compromises being made that are sometimes difficult or even impossible to fully understand, let alone translate consistently, and what's especially hard is adapting texts for media releases, which is something new they've given me to do, additional work – it's right up your alley, they said, so it makes sense; but it's getting to be all the same here – politics, the media, art, Renata said, to say nothing of the fact that I've had my fill of evening receptions, diplomatic audiences, nightclubs, even English, which is turning into a language of rented kitchens and public toilets, she said, although I've always loved it, ever since school, and I'm not sorry I studied it, even as a secondary subject, she said; after all, you can't get anywhere without languages, she said, but when I've been away from home for a long time, especially in this town, it seems like the only reason we learn English is so that, in an emergency, we can people our loneliness with it, patch over the gaps and distances between us, she said; you know, I'm so grateful for those times when I'm by myself and can lie back and read Slovene in silence; I don't know, but I feel like that's when I hear myself again, she said; not everything can be captured from one language into another, the story maybe, but not, well, I don't know . . . she said and ran a finger over the rim of her glass; so keep writing – always and everywhere keep writing, she said; I nodded and gave her a friendly smile, not unlike our patient, smiling waiter earlier; we're just people, that's all, she said. I didn't say anything. Let's eat, I don't have much time, she said and held her glass out to me across the table; come on, let's toast, say *na zdravje*; *na zdravje*, Renata, I said.

But now I am here, sitting at the top of these wide white steps; above me, a gentle slope, and above that, only sky, beneath which the royal palace, placed there long ago, stands lost in thought – marble portals, colonnades and terraced gardens, with the mundane traffic of cars and buses circling around them; a tram sounds its bell and sparks crackle on the electric cables as it starts up the hill on the other side of the wide avenue. Lower down, and nearer to my back, are museums and galleries, paintings, great canvases, sculptures and reliefs – beauty, which still remains silent, still clings convulsively to the earth as if to that hollow, darkening ball suspended on thin translucent cords from the cumulus clouds. I feel as if the celestial ball has started swinging, ringing, deep inside a dungeon, or that the strings are out of tune, the cords too taut for the high notes, they could snap at any moment, the fading echo of a certain period – the words slipped into my mind from somewhere; I remembered seeing them on a banner strung across a street, an advertisement and invitation for an exhibition at the National Museum in Ljubljana. The echo is fading, I thought, like the words the mysterious woman had addressed to me after my reading the evening before, at the Passa Porta bookshop.

I stood and read a few of my sentences: *I rode around Sobota a long time, looking for my sister Gerti. It was as though I was invisible, only a soul, eternally wandering. The town was asleep; it had fallen into a long, dreamless sleep; the houses on the main road were empty, nailed shut with boards; in the distance I heard soft singing, or maybe it was just the wind looking for a path between the houses, shifting the family photographs around in the abandoned flats, ruffling the cold sheets, drying tears, or maybe just waking guilty consciences, chilling hearts, which in spite of everything were still able to sleep. I turned on to the road for the synagogue; a light was flickering in the blue stained windows; I could feel that this was possibly my last night. Soldiers were in the yard. The Sobota*

above a graveyard,
were talking.

Jews who had been rounded up were sitting on their suitcases, their last luggage, which in the morning would go with them to the Auschwitz concentration camp, where I now lie slain in the snow. I am a soul; nobody can see me; nobody can do anything to me; all I want is to find my dear sister, Gerti; then we will disappear for ever from this world, I thought and turned into the yard in front of the synagogue. I rode between the soldiers; nobody moved; I rang the bell; I pushed open the guarded door with my bicycle and rode straight inside, where a blue light was shining as if the sky had come down to the earth. I was riding between people – they were lying on the floor, standing, weeping, silent; somebody was playing a violin; others were humming – maybe that was the song the wind was carrying through the town – but she wasn't there; my Gerti wasn't among them. I turned back to the door and rode out to the street. What if she had gone back to that dead garden, was waiting for me in the cold shed, alone, had forgotten something important there, a photograph in a suitcase, a letter, money, a watch, god knows what, or simply didn't want to keep running, and so now was waiting for me there? I was sure of it. Thank you, I said and sat down.

Unfortunately, I don't know your language and can't understand it, but I can feel the way you tell your story, the lady said; it's hard for me to talk about it in a foreign language, I apologize, but I understand that you're writing about sadness and the past; I just wanted to tell you this, please don't be offended, she said and quietly slipped away, disappearing into the bookshelves, I remember. I was smoking in the passageway in front of the bookshop when she approached me again in a kind, friendly manner; the people who had attended the reading were leaving and I was waiting for Pavel, who still had a few things to take care of, and a small group of Slovenes who worked in the city, so we could go on somewhere else. I'd just like to share my story with you, if I may; I know that no story is the same, and you are still young, the woman said and lit a cigarette, but even so; we're meeting at L'Archiduc, at the end of the street, they had told me – come by later, we have a reservation. Allow me, the woman said; I took two glasses, the last ones – they'll be cleaning up soon; thank you, I said, cheers. I remember, although I never talk about it, she told me as we walked slowly through the passageway to the street, there were years when I was happy, when I thought that all you needed was to forget, to live for today; I fell in love with a foreigner when I was very young – Mama said I went to bed with the first stranger who came to Mechelen, but that's not true, she said and put the glass down on the pavement; the evening was damp and chilly; I kept shifting my feet, which were cold in my lightweight shoes; let's walk a little, I'll take you to where your friends are waiting for you, she said; I nodded; Mama knew nothing about life, nothing at all, or maybe she was simply trying hard to forget everything, to hide it inside herself, she said; I'm just like her, the very same; I had the idea that the happiness I was looking for in men would allow me to escape everything my mother had had to put up with; I don't know, she said; we were walking down the street slowly; she had taken my arm and slowed her pace to light a cigarette; I know, she said, I remember, Mama told me when I returned after years of crazy trips with my crazy husband – he played the clarinet and everything was crazy in those years, let me tell you – jazz, movies, being young; it was the only way I could forget the war, forget my father, and forget provincial Mechelen, the only way I could bury my childhood and the crime I was forced to witness with my own eyes, she said; oh yes, he bewitched me with his music; he used to play here, too, she said when we were standing in front of L'Archiduc; they had the best jazz in Brussels here, she said and pressed her head to the window; sometimes we had to listen to the music from here; they'd have the door open; I would watch him through the window, watch him

play, it was crazy; I don't know what he was thinking about then; he'd look at me but I know he didn't see me; he had a faraway look in his eye; he won me with that look, those quick fingers running up and down the black clarinet; I knew I would never have him entirely to myself, he would always be somewhere else, far away and alone, like his crazy music; he would kill us both with his freedom, but I never had his strength; I stayed in the background, and just ten years later it put him in the grave; he wasn't afraid; he went wherever the music went, he said, she said; should I tell you? she said and looked at me; I nodded and shifted my weight; the traffic was standing still, the cars waiting in a long line, headlights gleaming in the fine drizzle; the pavement in front of the club was crowded, women in light coats, men in business suits, everyone with a beer in their hand and a cigarette; they were laughing and looking at pictures on their phones; yes, she said and slowly exhaled the grey cigarette smoke, I was five years old; my father worked on the railway – he was a conductor; every day he'd ride the local Brussels–Mechelen–Antwerp line, leaving early in the morning and returning in the evening; he always carried a big leather bag and wore a cap with a badge; sometimes he'd bring us something – waffles, chocolate or a big bottle of cherry beer; he would put everything on the table and I would be given a little bit of it and then sent to bed; I never ate anything right away; I guarded it all, hid it under the mattress, put it in the wardrobe with my shoes and even buried it in the garden behind the house; I remember a beat-up, scratched-up, light-blue box with a big six-pointed yellow star on the lid; I put biscuits in it, hard candies, half a piece of chocolate, a photograph from my baptism, she said; Mama could barely hold me in her arms – I hadn't been a baby in a long time; I was wrapped in a white quilted blanket, so I never saw my childish face; my father stood to the side, in the shadow of the pulpit, somewhat aloof and withdrawn; he held a small white candle and stared into the empty nave of the church; at least I imagine we were alone, that nobody was watching us; it was probably the priest who took our picture since he's not in the photo himself, she said; Father was dressed in his regular railway uniform, holding his big bag in the other hand; the ceremony had been held during work hours, or maybe after work, late at night, in secret, she said; much later, when there was nobody left who could tell me, I found out, the woman said and peeked through the window into the club; could you wait here a moment, please? There's somebody I know in there, she said and vanished through the door. I was saying hello to Tomaž and his wife, both Slovenes, who were already leaving, when the woman returned with two big glasses of beer; I'm thirsty, I've been talking too much, she said. I wasn't even twenty and already I'd been all over Paris, and Rome, and the divided Berlin; I celebrated my birthday just a few days after Marc and I – that was the name of my clarinettist – after we stepped off the boat in New York; that was his homeland, but there was no place he really felt at home there; we were always travelling and moving; we'd stay a few months somewhere if there was an opening in a jazz band, or if he had a contract to play in a club, hotel or school, but then we were on the run again – from unpaid bills, angry musicians or hotel owners. He would tell me stories, the woman said, about his family, who he'd left behind as early as

I had mine; he couldn't stand poverty, nostalgia or reading out loud, she said and emptied her glass. He was the third son of Ukrainian immigrants; we're Jewish, he said – but I didn't want to understand that; I was young, in love, and wanted to forget, to become the wife of an American, a crazy clarinet player's woman, and nothing else, just that, she said. We met in Brussels, which is where I would escape from home by train in the evening; he came to Europe to study and to play in a small band; all I remember is the rain, nothing but the rain; we sat until morning on the steps of the Bourse, kissing; he didn't want to play any more, we'd just kiss; it was the only language we had in common. Mama saw him only once, when she came to see me off at the station in Mechelen; Marc was waiting for me there, so we could leave; I heard him right away, he was playing on the platform, improvising, crazy stuff, she said; I knew it, I always told your father you don't know how to keep secrets, it will all come floating up behind you, Mama said when she saw him, when she heard him, she said and dropped her cigarette on the wet pavement; this was the first time Mama had ever heard jazz improv and she never would again; she stood there a while, then put my suitcase down on the platform and left the station without even greeting him, returning to her sadness and loneliness, to her oblivion.

Among the shapes in the evening air that were descending and slowly ascending Mont des Arts, in no perceivable pattern, people coming with slow steps down the parallel, symmetrically designed footpaths, through the scrupulously tended tree-lined park with a fountain at one end, I recognized her as she stepped on to the white steps and her figure separated from the crowd of random promenaders with whom I was sharing the dwindling of the light. I had met her in Mons on my previous, my first, trip to Belgium – we shared space behind a table on a stage; the discussion was more or less delineated by the general topic and bore the title 'A Reassuring Foreignness', which attempted to encapsulate the elusive and indefinable ideas of space and

the writer's experience; I don't have my own landscape, I search for
and invent the spaces of my language, Caroline had said; I was born
here, but I took my first steps and spoke my first words – which, sadly,
I later forgot – in Spain, where I spent my early childhood; I studied
Romance languages and my work took me to Paris, and later I taught
French for a few years in Nigeria; even there my pupils had never
known, and would possibly never know, any experience of a foreign
space; for them, that did not exist, she had said; people can learn a
different language, one that in their actual experience does not belong
to any space, that exists only on a map in school, in textbooks and,
truly, only in the throat and heart of each individual speaker, she had
said and picked up a piece of paper from the table; a few weeks ago

I returned from a long stay in Maribor, where I had been invited, she had said; I'd like to read some of the notes I made, she had said and started reading, slowly: *an elderly woman and her daughter come out of a building on which I have been admiring a piece of graffiti in the shape of a bird. We all go for coffee together and the old woman speaks to me in French. She tells me that her father was from Maribor but he worked in the mines in northern France. And that's where she was born, in 1923. At the start of the Second World War her parents made her go back to Slovenia. The French will always be foreigners to us, they told her. So at the age of seventeen she began to discover Maribor, the cradle of her family; she soon married, but when she was forty, she lost her husband. Her daughter, too, became a widow, years ago. The daughter does not speak French, but she listens to us with an almost supernatural sweetness. The old woman's French is fluent; it's as if she had never stopped speaking it all these years. In her pink sweater, she is charmingly elegant. She has a bandaged eye; she was recently operated on for cataracts. Her daughter wears a scarf on her head; beneath it you can sense a new growth of downy hair. Chemotherapy. I gathered that the prognosis is not promising, which is all the more reason for her to enjoy every brief moment of pleasure, such as our meeting.* And now just a few more lines, Caroline had said: *Two days before I left, a gentleman named Branko rounded out this series of unexpected encounters in a very meaningful way. I go up to him that evening and ask if he knows of a shortcut through the vineyards (where we had met) that would take me to the ruins of the old castle. No, he says, you have to go all the way down to the park and then up the other hill. During our conversation he tells me that this very evening, at nine o'clock, there will be a lunar eclipse. He is too tired to go with me all the way to Pyramid Hill, but he escorts me to the park; as we walk, he tells me that at the age of sixty-two he still works in administration, while his university-educated thirty-year-old son is unemployed. In his opinion, the government should not be extending the employment period but should shorten it so that young people can find jobs. He adds that he, too, prefers Maribor to Ljubljana, where he worked for a time. He was born in Maribor and will die in Maribor.*

Even if the city has lost its shine, even if some of its beautiful houses are falling apart. There's nothing you can do to stop it; it's just how it is. We shake hands. I ask him his name, and he asks me mine. What a coincidence – my wife is named Karolina, and so is my sister. Then, at a more leisurely pace, he makes his way home, while I make mine to the hill people call the Pyramid. Walking up the hill, I meet many who are hoping to see the eclipse. At nine o'clock it is still quite light out, but even so, we can see the lunar eclipse: the moon becomes gradually smaller; it flickers, thinner and thinner, above the railway tracks, where every so often a train rumbles by on the regular line between Vienna and Zagreb. In the distance, you can also sense the river, which disappears between the mountains into the night. After the terrible heat of the day, it has finally become a little cooler.

She had put the paper down on the table along with a pair of tiny eyeglasses; I think . . . she had said in the semidarkness and silence that hovered beneath the ceiling of the former industrial plant – I remember how, hanging in place of ordinary lights, there were some elaborate multi-coloured arrangements of discarded plastic soft drink bottles with electric candles stuck inside them, which cast a discreet light across people's faces; the hall had only recently been converted into a café, I was told – well, I think, Caroline had said, that the idea of some inner bond between language and place is still alive for most people, it's still a given, something eternal and immutable; I would say that it was their only tangible identity, but for many this bond has been broken, or lost, or seemingly transcended – many people, painfully and sometimes tragically, are forced, or for pragmatic reasons desire and are able, to transcend and break this bond; consider, she had said, people who are immigrants, refugees, the various diasporas, and so I ask myself what is still left to the writer's experience. Nothing, she said now, when we met again after several months, nothing is left; this city, now that Robert, my one and only friend, is gone, is empty for me; it's as though all at once the city became foreign to me and, mainly, inexplicably cold; sometimes in the late afternoon when I take my usual walk, my stroll along the familiar streets, to the regular places I go at that time of day, the little shops, the *chocolateries*, where I carefully pick out some small gift for my daughter and little grand-daughter, which I send them by post or take with me when I visit them in London – that's when this feeling gets stronger inside me, that I am really homeless, she said, as we walked downhill to the centre of town, past Gare Centrale, which by now was fully illuminated – a yellowish light was filtering from the train station's interior, which was clad in marble and stone with a large memorial inscription on the wall, cast in bronze and dedicated to the unknown hero – to all who died for their country, it says, I remembered; the square in front of the entrance, lined with black and white pillars, which now were similarly lit by spotlights, was unusually barren, I thought; we crossed it, and no more than a few people walked past; the only noise came from the newspa-per sellers and people with mugs of beer who, after working late in the office, were now standing on the pavement in front of the pubs and smoking cigarettes; I'm going to Antwerp in the morning, I said; are you staying there? she asked; no, I said, I want to have a look at the train station and walk around the city, and see the Jewish quarter – a woman I met in Ghent will be meeting me, I said; when I'm in Antwerp what I like doing most is going outside the city, she said; I drive far out into the suburbs and keep going, through the empty, windy area by the Scheldt River and all the way to its wide mouth, to the port. I think that at least once I managed to walk the whole endless stretch of the coast, where there are dozens of miles of docks with tall cranes, tugboats, mobile elevators on tracks, very long and especially very boring warehouses and storehouses, enormous, high and closely guarded container depots surrounded by barbed wire, which in many places, however, has been cut and is rusty and drooping – places you could walk through with a clean conscience and, if you have no goal or purpose, lose your way, Caroline said; from a distance, the half-deserted container depots in the old section of the port look like honeycombs, or maybe a rusted-out jetty, or the endless iron curtain Europe is again wrapping around itself, she said, I don't know any more who it's meant to keep out, the sea maybe, maybe the infinite

abyss inside us, she said; I like the edges of these devastated places, the cries of the birds that sit on the docks and peck through the rubbish; sometimes I would hear the disturbing cry of some tropical bird I didn't recognize – that's another thing I learned from my friend Robert, when he was still taking me there; he knew birds; he recognized their cries – thin, deep, high, screeching, pulsating, she said; it's strange, she said, I always thought I respected and valued him because he was my best, my favourite, bookseller in the city, in the world, she said; now that he's no longer among his bookshelves, which he was always organizing, rearranging and filling, I only hear his absent voice there, like an invisible bird; I see everything differently now, I hear what I didn't see before, Caroline said; we had been pacing and smoking a while in front of the Galeries Royales Saint-Hubert, as if hesitating, trying to decide whether or not to go in. It was already quite dark out – above the streets, with their floodlit shop windows below and the squares and lines of illuminated flats on top, was a dark-blue, partly cloudy but still not totally black evening sky; do you remember? Caroline said; we had finally extinguished our cigarettes and stepped inside the long shopping arcade, which was covered by a lightweight lattice-like construction of glass and iron; beneath it, a soft warm light was seeping slowly out of the display windows of tiny confectioneries, tailor shops and fashion boutiques, stationers, pubs, old cinemas, bookbinders and galleries, but mainly it issued from the bodies, the thoughts, the languages dressed in overcoats, which were coming and going; yes, I remember, I said; this is where we came to see your friend Robert – it was on my first trip here, and the next morning I had to fly home, I said; that evening, I remember, Robert was pacing back and forth in front of his bookshop; yes, he was waiting for us, he knew we were coming, I told him I was bringing a guest, she said as we examined the titles of the books in the window display. Even in the damp and foggy air radiant with the diffuse light over the broad river, Robert could recognize a tiny lost bird that had flown all the way to the far north, Caroline said and peered into the shadows of the shop, where only tiny white lights were still dimly burning above the solid-wood shelves of what used to be apothecary cabinets; a tiny bespectacled woman sat behind a desk putting receipts in order; no, she merely shook her head when we desired to enter; we understood: she was closing. On that earlier occasion, Robert had let us into the bookshop and immediately switched off the big light above the tables stacked with heavy monographs, books on art history and exhibition catalogues; I used to specialize, fine art – that's my area; look around and choose something, he had said and walked over to the door and locked the shop. Let's go upstairs, he had said after a while, and then turned off the computer and locked the cash register; I'll take this – *Panorama*, I had said, after we climbed the narrow winding stairs to his little office, which looked out on an empty, unlit inner courtyard; I saw the Richter retrospective in London – that's when it was published, he had said and wrapped up the book for me in stiff black paper; here you go, he had said and cleared the coffee table of its piles of papers, book orders, catalogues, opened books, bottles and posters and then cheerfully opened a new bottle of red wine; up here it's still possible to live, he had said, lying back on the couch; we all lit our cigarettes; even if it keeps getting harder down below; for many people, books are too heavy now – whole flocks used to come to the shop, but now it's just the occasional lonely bird who stops by and takes the time to browse through the books, even hours at a time, like my friend Caroline, he had said and smiled; he recognized that little lost bird, Caroline said; we were still standing hopelessly in front of the closed bookshop; he knew every bird that by some miracle had survived the long voyage on one of the thousands of tankers and ocean liners that drop anchor a few miles offshore; they sit there, on the still horizon, always waiting for high tide, for the right water level, so they can sail into the mouth of the river, to the docks, where we would watch them for hours and hours; because out there, when you get away from the port, from the river, the ships and the cranes, she said and paused for a moment; when you step carefully through the tall grass into the soft and soggy ground, which has an unusual smell to it, of oil, the sea, life, you soon feel, even though everything really is degraded and devastated,

that in this remote and distant silence there is still an unknown poem hiding, possibly only birdsong – wounded, frightened, lost and alien, but for us it was miraculously beautiful.

It's all true, what she told me, only I can't make anything right again; Jane is gone; this is how it happened, Gjini said as we sat on a metal bench on the platform drinking coffee from paper cups; not long after that night when I was frightened I wouldn't find her back at the house where we were spending the night, I never saw her again, Gjini said as we waited for our respective trains, which were leaving at more or less the same time, at ten o'clock; we still had a little more than an hour; Gospođa Spomenka was meeting me at the station in Antwerp at eleven. I came back with the bucket of water; I was hurrying, but even so, I didn't spill much, Gjini said; even from far away I could see the glow from the fireplace in the night; I thought it must be warm up there by now and that Jane had made tea using the water in the flask; I quickened my pace, he said and, standing up from the bench, took a step towards the tracks; I found her on the floor – she was lying there with a piece of bread and loose sugar clenched in her fist, he said; I put the bucket down and wet her face and neck; I knew she needed sugar; we hadn't eaten anything the whole day, he said; we were travelling, you and me, Jane said moments later, when she came to; she drank some sugared water and ate a piece of cheese; the bread in our bag we divided. She didn't talk, but I could sense that she wanted to tell me something; we were both tired, exhausted. We lay down on the wooden bed, on the bare boards; the fire was gradually dying down, and we watched the murky, reddish shadows it cast, nothing else; I could feel that she was about to fall asleep, but she didn't relax her embrace, Gjini said; we were walking slowly down the long underground platform next to the tracks, and I could feel that he was no longer in a rush to be anywhere, even if the clock was ticking, the trains departing in rapid order, one after another; only the embers were still glowing, he said and stopped in his tracks, when Jane suddenly lifted herself in the darkness and said, I mustn't stop, I have to go on, Gjini said and continued on towards the escalator; as he descended, he waved to me from the crowd of people, who were travelling on.

The evening before, when I renewed my acquaintance with Caroline, after we took our short stroll through the Galeries Royales we had a beer at À la Mort Subite, a pub across the street and just a few steps from the exit at the opposite end of the arcade. Robert used to come here in the evening after he locked up the bookshop and I'd go with him, or sometimes I would wait for him here; I was trying to write; it's quiet here in the afternoon, just the occasional tourist or elderly couple, she said; I was writing radio plays; that's still how I make my living, but I can't write in the city any more; in fact, I've almost stopped writing altogether, she said. A noisy group of tourists came in and sat down at a long wooden table in the middle of the room;

they raised their arms so the waiter could count them; we were sitting behind the door, our backs against a vaulted brick wall; let's leave; I need to go home, I'm having supper with my husband tonight; he just got back from a long business trip and we hardly ever see each other, Caroline said; the walls were covered in large pictures with carved gold frames – merchants, bankers and politicians, all painted or photographed in dark sports jackets and holding newspapers, cigars and beer mugs; at the opposite end of the pub, the well-polished tap handles, brass, white and black, were reflected on the surface of the bar; office workers, secretaries and functionaries were arriving after finishing a long workday; they sat down at separate tables in a corner on the other side of the room with their tablets and phones in front of them, browsing the web or reading; the chandeliers were switched on; light and soft semidarkness, heavy evening traffic outside, buses, trams, fast cars and, among them, pedestrians with umbrellas going down the street, it's crowded and they're in a hurry. We stepped on to the pavement and our table by the window was already occupied. People were waiting beneath the eaves to be let into the pub. We said goodbye; Caroline walked to the metro; I took the long way back to my hotel and got soaked. In the lobby, hotel guests were sitting on red-cushioned benches, but it was still strangely quiet, as if no one was there; they were all absorbed in the computers and tablets on their laps, whispering over Skype and checking mails; I joined them, got connected to the hotel's network, retrieved my email and uploaded a few photos to Facebook. I saw at once that Gjini had finally answered, after three days. He wrote me that he had caught the train to Ypres at the last possible second, arrived in a terrible downpour, and that the city seemed dark and alien to him, even though it had been completely rebuilt after the First World War; he wrote that he now understood what Jane was trying to tell him when she said the city had never recovered its soul; he had spent the night with friends and the next morning tried to locate and photograph the site in the city, on the former rue Saint-Jacques, where there had once been a convent run by Irish nuns, the order of the Irish Dames of Ypres, who had been there since the seventeenth century; after a few clicks on the web, I discovered a fair number of old photographs of the building on the street he had mentioned; some had been taken when the complex was still standing there peacefully and serving its noble purpose, but the last photograph was just a picture of its ruins, a memorial to its destruction.

The convent was founded primarily for the aid, care and education of young Irish girls, the daughters, of course, of wealthy parents who wished to send their darling children abroad – and did so in particularly large numbers during the time of the Great Famine, which in the middle of the nineteenth century was killing off the Irish like the plague, Gjini wrote; I'll cover this in more detail in my article. Sadly, in 1914, in the very first months of the war, the convent, like the rest of that unfortunate city, was razed to the ground; the Germans bombed it even from the air. The woman who kept the Benedictine sisters from despair and guided their spiritual lives was, by the grace of God, as the nuns said, the Lady Abbess Scholastica Berg, a Belgian by birth; sources report that at the time she herself was terribly ill and unable to walk. At her urging and with her emotional support, the sisters that same year, just a few months after the annihilation, made their difficult and seemingly desperate decision and, abandoning the ashes of their centuries-old home, left the city on foot. They took with them on their journey only a few precious items of furniture and some devotional images, which they had managed to keep safe for a time in the cellar beneath the ruins, and each sister had her own tiny prayer book with her. They walked in a tight column, carrying their abbess, Sister Scholastica, in their arms and singing and praying all the way to Paris, 280 miles in total, which by my calculations would have taken them a good week to walk, Gjini wrote; I'll be including this detail in my article as an illustration for the reader. Jane would speak about this compulsory pilgrimage, this human ordeal in a world gone mad, where, she said, neither wolves nor devils nor angels could survive, in a way that was unusually vivid and poignant, Gjini wrote; I feel that I myself am sister to these sisters, Jane said. Despite a few attempts on the part of the Benedictine nuns to return to Ypres, the battlefront, where the armies had positioned themselves along the Franco-Belgian border in mile upon mile of trenches, made this impossible. After the apocalypse they had endured, they decided to leave for ever the bleeding soil of Europe and retreat to England, where they sought a temporary refuge that might allow them to resume their educational mission in peace, Gjini wrote, but in England, too, there was no room for the homeless nuns and soon they moved again, this time to Ireland, just as their brothers had done a thousand years earlier when they fled from the collapse of the empire, Gjini wrote. The Benedictine sisters found shelter and consolation in a small, remote convent where, two years later, Sister Scholastica Berg died in peace and hope. Her last whispered wish was that here, on their home soil, her sisters would again build themselves a house and in it spread knowledge, faith and good breeding. The nuns laid their departed abbess to rest in a modest grave and marked it with the heavy stone cross she had borne faithfully all her life. In these uncertain and disheartening conditions, the leadership of the community was then assumed by Lady Abbess Maura Ostyn, another Belgian by birth, who soon left on a solitary journey through this foreign land, intending at last to find a suitable permanent home for her devoted Benedictine sisterhood; I assume, wrote Gjini, that Sister Maura travelled first from Dublin to Galway, and then on to Clifden, by train, which in those days was a very modern and also, in a way, quite ordinary thing to do – when I realized this, and for some reason I had initially overlooked it, I felt the same unusual yearning that would always come over Jane when, on our car trips, she'd talk to me nostalgically about the trains; she could hardly compose herself when she learned that in 1930, in the years after independence, it was the Irish themselves who had destroyed all the train tracks and burned down the village stations on the Galway–Clifden line, which has never been restored; for them, that line was a painful and all too obvious remnant of the English imperialism

they wished to vanquish for ever, Gjini wrote, but as you know, he wrote me, the line was built primarily to serve the needs of Marconi's telegraph station, which, sadly, was something else they laid waste to in that turbulent year, burning it to the ground, Gjini wrote. The wooden structure with its big antennas stood just a few miles from Clifden, above the sea in the middle of barren land; Jane told me there was a memorial there now – it was the first destination point she went to on her walking trips, I remember Gjini telling me when he took me to Clifden in his red Toyota. The next day, when I rented the bike and was cycling through the town and in the surrounding area, I discovered the memorial, which tells of the historic moment in 1905 when the engineer Guglielmo Marconi succeeded in establishing the first regular wireless telegraph connection between Europe and North America, more precisely, between Clifden and Nova Scotia; it's crazy, unbelievable, Jane said when we lay next to the memorial bathing in the sunlight and peering into the azure expanses, at the sea whose waves were breaking against the distant shores of her home,

Gjini said; from this very spot, to which I would journey so many days and nights, if only in my confused thoughts and dreams and crazy hopes, as if sensing an invisible bond to these lonely, wild, storm-tossed shores, these cliffs, these green plains and abandoned homes, from this spot, from this wasteland, even before I was born, someone was able, for the first time in history, to transmit a signal across the Atlantic, Jane said, a message that, nevertheless, when I am sitting by the sea beneath my cliffs, I still innocently associate with the Atlantic Gulf Stream, with long waves, wind and birds that carry hidden omens, Jane wrote in her journal, which I read later, much later; well, that's all I'll say for now about the dilemmas and topics that occupy me, Gjini told me in his letter. He wrote: So now I can say with certainty that Lady Abbess Maura Ostyn travelled by train to the station in Clifden, and then probably, in the cheerful company of a solicitor, surveyor and the attorney for the seller, who had all been waiting impatiently for her on the platform, she went by car on the narrow macadamized road, the same one that today goes to Kylemore Abbey, through twists and turns, across hills and peatlands, over bogs and pastures, into the interior of what to her was still a mysterious and in its own way terrible and fascinating but certainly utterly alien and unusual landscape, as Sister Maura might well have been thinking during the drive, Gjini said. I can imagine her long, slow journey, Jane writes; Lady Abbess Maura was a foreigner, a Belgian, even in a sense a refugee, who here was searching for her home, for a house for all of us, just as I myself, here again, am searching for my forgotten name, Jane wrote in her journal, the one I was carrying in my bag.

I went outside to the street and lit a cigarette in front of the hotel; it was drizzling; a translucent mist lay over the city, which was not sleeping but merely dozing, rapidly processing other people's dreams. I walked down rue du Cyprès, the shadowy one-way street that ran alongside the hotel; there was nobody in the park across the street; the sounds of laughter and talk hovering in the damp air had escaped into the night through somebody's open balcony doors beyond the park somewhere, the light blocked by leafy trees whose crowns reached past

the rooftops. Taking the side street rue du Peuplier, I came to the open, spacious square in front of St Catherine's Church, which was asleep, blanketed in scaffolding and enormous protective sheets; the last guests, probably, were leaving the seafood restaurant on the corner; they were smoking and taking pictures with their phones. Spread out above us, the sky was smothered in low dense cloud, although bright from the glow of the city lights in the distance below. It had stopped raining and, for a moment, the city traffic was still. I went back to the hotel and, in my room, continued reading: Deep in the bleak, poor, raw but beautiful Connemara landscape, surrounded by mountains, beneath a blue sky, mirrored in the lake, Maura Ostyn found Kylemore Castle, which had been deserted – the castle's last owners (by then the key had exchanged hands several times) were a profligate English couple given to cards and alcohol, and after their financial ruin the castle stood empty, abandoned to slow and persistent decay – but long before, it had had a mighty and glorious past, forged by the visionary spirit, dedication and hard work, and especially the deep,

extraordinary love that the first owners of the estate and castle, an English couple named Margaret and Henry Mitchell, had invested in it. With the help of the Church and the faithful, the Benedictine sisters soon collected the necessary funds and bought the castle, along with its extensive land, outbuildings and an enormous walled Victorian garden. On that first visit, Lady Abbess Maura Ostyn had walked with delight through the abandoned garden entirely alone, while her companions waited for her in a heated room, in the cottage where the chief gardener had once lived with his family; with tumblers of the excellent local whisky in their hands, they merely observed her through a grimy window, warmed by thoughts of a good sale as they watched Maura move slowly and thoughtfully through the garden, in her black robe and veil, despite the rain and wind, which announced the end of the warm autumn; perhaps that was the moment, as she contemplated the dry flowers, the fallen leaves and branches, the unpruned shrubbery, the filthy benches, the neglected overgrown paths, when she made up her mind; she was particularly taken, and at the same time pained, when she saw the dilapidated covered gardens, her solicitor said later, for when she had managed with some difficulty to at last open the broken glass door, she had stood there speechless, peering inside. The muddy and mouldering long tables were covered in cracked or broken clay pots; withered, rotting stems were hanging from the ceiling; empty beer and whisky bottles were everywhere to be seen; herbaria, seed calendars, handbooks with translations of Latin botanical terms, garden sketches and building plans and piles of soggy paper bags with ruined seeds lay scattered across the tables and on the ground; so that's when she must have decided, as she lingered there watching the slow rain, the rain that had been falling into the glasshouse for years through the broken windows in the roof, that's when she must have decided to bring life back to this land through the power of her love, faith and hope. Only later, after years of hard work, did Maura gradually remove the veils that had covered, had jealously guarded, the past love and tragedy from which everything here had been created. It was only then, years later, when life was already slowly but surely returning, after the manor had been restored by diligent labourers and virtuous house assistants from the local villages, that Lady Abbess Maura Ostyn would often hear people describe how the garden had once boasted the most modern heated glasshouses, which in the golden days had produced food not only for the family at the manor and their numerous servants but also for the hundred or more workers who came to the estate every day. In the glasshouses and outside garden plots the most exotic plants had once grown, sent here from all over the world by horticulturalists, botanists and florists – all of it Maura managed to reconstruct from the salvaged journals of the lord of the manor and the diaries of his manager. Margaret and Henry had sown, crossbred and given names to many seeds and seedlings here; they cultivated them with their own soft, white, loving hands; Jane said that the moment she first entered this miraculous garden, which at the time was again in full bloom, Gjini said – it was mid-June and the young blossoms of the many aromatic margarets and henrys were floating on the sweet air, or at least that's how I imagined it, Jane said, as I sat by a wall in the shade, admiring the restored garden with my eyes closed, which was growing and blossoming, Jane wrote in her journal – at that moment something accepted me, it was as if somebody had given me my life back, Jane wrote later.

Many of the seeds and seedlings had been brought back by the couple from their long travels in exotic places – such trips in those days were greatly valued in high society; a particularly favourite destination for both the old English aristocracy and the fast-growing circles of the young capitalist bourgeoisie and polite middle class was pharaonic Egypt. This was a time when many of those who had managed to win financial freedom and extract themselves from the bonds of society – in short, who had successfully severed the Gordian knot of faith and tradition – were suddenly possessed by the reawakened passion for travel, for uncovering the spiritual mysteries that had once been reported by pilgrims, missionaries and seafarers. But now, joining such travellers, there were also more than a few notorious adventurers who desired only fame, eccentric poets and quite ordinary vagabonds whose half-imaginary stories about amazing natural phenomena, the bloodthirstiness of the dark-skinned races and paradisiacal landscapes, which, of course, were hidden from eyes and hearts in the terrible remote lands of the East and the Far South, on the margins of the still barely charted world, conveyed the message that, while divine miracles may have vanished from the earth, the world was still full of the wonders of nature, which were waiting to be discovered and seen – so all these eternal wanderers, explorers, homeless wayfarers and eyewitnesses of questionable provenance filled the front and back pages of the ever more numerous press with countless illustrated features, alarming news reports, versified epics and doubtful scientific theories, which inflamed the imaginations and passions of bored and jaded Europeans. To travel, to see, to experience – suddenly this was the only thing, apart from the latest fashions and their recent purchases, that people were talking about, loudly, enthusiastically and authoritatively, in the company of their peers; as it happened, our own dear couple, the parents of nine children and the proud masters of Kylemore Castle, Margaret and Henry Mitchell, found themselves among them, inadvertently surrendering to the general mania for travel. In the spring or early summer of 1874 they left on a well-deserved and much-anticipated holiday to exotic Egypt. In the middle of this romantic journey, which Margaret had vocally been dreaming about, the lady unexpectedly took ill. It happened during a slow boat trip on the Nile, after she and her husband had inspected the pyramids in Giza; the doctor, who was unable to see her until their return to Cairo, could only confirm a severe bacterial infection, to which Margaret, despite her devout wish to be able for many years still, on those long, cold evenings in the heated manor, to recount her impressions to her children, soon succumbed. Despairing and emotionally shattered, Henry travelled home with his beloved wife; I cannot leave you here in this cold foreign soil, he said. Immediately on his return to Kylemore Castle, the unhappy widower set to work on a large and carefully planned construction project: not far from

the manor, he had a chapel erected to honour his dear one, a small-scale Gothic cathedral, which was intended as a testimony to their eternal loyalty and to a love that never dies.

So to sum up – Gjini wrote in his letter to me – Maura Ostyn, having arrived there after her long and harrowing journey from the annihilated, lost convent in Ypres, after her pilgrimage to Paris and then on to London, Dublin, Galway and finally Clifden, and seeing for the first time the ravaged gardens and deserted manor with its large property, which stretched far and wide across the surrounding hills, lakes, empty meadows, peat bogs, pasturelands and raging rivers – a property one cannot fully cover in a single day, not even in a modern automobile, Maura Ostyn said – instantly decided in her heart, and this inner voice was confirmed by her clear-thinking head, that she and her sisters would purchase Kylemore Castle. Within its damp, faded but once magnificent walls, covered in oil paintings and, especially, family photographs – portraits, landscapes and still lifes, all developed in the master's own darkroom – in these luxurious chambers, among the chairs and long tables, sofas and divans, which had been draped in heavy sheets and oilcloths when the honourable sisters arrived, a wind began to blow; in the cold fireplaces and musty kitchen, where nothing had been cooked for a very long time, a fire was suddenly crackling again; in short, the house, which was now also a house of God, had been given new life, as the sisters said; with love, faith and hope, the honourable nuns soon transformed the manor into a convent – Kylemore Abbey, which is still their home today, Gjini wrote. And in 1923, just two short years after their arrival, the Benedictine sisters opened an international boarding school in the now well-ventilated, whitewashed and converted manor, and for many decades, right up until 2010, girls from all over Europe, and even from Japan and America, would come here in search of faith, good breeding and knowledge, Gjini wrote; I remember what it was like that year, it was the first time I came here, Jane told me when she was later showing me around; by then, the classrooms and large dormitories in the boarding school were empty; they had just been cleaning them for the last time and putting away all the files, Jane said; we were walking through the empty rooms, which echoed with our every step, our slightest word, as if the voices of the girls were still there, Gjini said; afterwards, Jane and I climbed the hill behind the manor to see the view; we took our time, walking slowly and sitting a while on the steep grassy slope; I remember we were going down on the other side towards the lake just before evening, Gjini said, when Jane took my hand and led me to that old, heavy stone cross; here, beneath this cross, which she bore with courage, Jane said, Maura is buried; she died in 1940, the year my father was born, Jane said; the kind nuns took me to the boat that was leaving for Canada; I was five years old – that's all he could tell me about the place he was born, Jane said, Gjini told me; you know how the story continues, he wrote; do you remember our trip? he asked me in his letter; yes, I remember, I thought. I sat there with the tablet in my lap, reading; it was still raining outside; I pulled the curtain open and shifted the sliding window; in the hotel's inner courtyard I saw a glimmer on the black asphalt and the glow of the street lamps. It was the way it had been a few months ago, in the early spring, when Gjini and I were walking along the narrow path by the lake. No reflection had been visible on the rippling surface, which was veiled in the shadows from the steep slopes of the surrounding hills; we're running late, Gjini had said; soon we won't be able to see a thing; let's at least take a look at the chapel; Jane adored it, she said; the first time she entered it, years ago, she at once had the feeling that this was the only place on earth she was safe; I could have stayed there, she said; the next day Gjini had returned to Brussels, again staying with friends, he wrote at the end of his letter; he had taken a short trip to nearby Mechelen; I went to the museum at the Kazerne Dossin, a former military barracks; during the war it had been a Nazi assembly camp from where they deported Belgian Jews to Auschwitz, Gjini wrote; I have visited all of her places; I wanted to see everything Jane saw; I feel shaken; I don't understand it, Gjini wrote. There were a number of important things I needed to take care of quickly; I'm running late with my article and have to send my editor a draft of the text they commissioned from me; that's why I haven't written until now. Tomorrow I fly home on Ryanair in the late afternoon; I'm taking the train from Gare Centrale to the airport; then I fly to Dublin, from where, for the first time in a long while, I'll be going by train to Galway; the last time I went by rail was with my wife and child, when after several years I had finally managed to arrange visas for my family; I remember meeting them at the station, after which we treated ourselves to our first trip together to our new home, as I told my wife, Gjini wrote. Before my flight I'd like to visit the Photography Museum in Charleroi; Jane warmly recommended it. The train from Brussels leaves every hour; I'll take the one between ten and eleven. Hotel Astrid, where you're staying, isn't far from the train station; I checked Google Maps; if you get this message in time, we can meet at the station, that's where I'll be; so I'll have to get up early, I thought, but I'll definitely be there; fortunately, we have trains at the same time; I go to Antwerp tomorrow, I thought. I will definitely tell you more when I see you, Gjini added.

P.S. You can do whatever you like with the journal.

But before her hosts and companions drove Lady Abbess Maura Ostyn back to Clifden, and after she had expressed her desire and willingness to try to collect the necessary money, and they all had shaken hands, Maura said: I must stay alone here tonight; only then will I put my name, and pledge the good name of my sisters, at the bottom of our agreement, Maura said, as Jane writes in her journal, which I was reading on my way to Antwerp: The gentlemen were silent for a moment; they lit their cigars again and, all together, peered out at the gloomy weather; the fire had gone out in the hearth in the gardener's cottage, the manor was draughty and damp, cold waves were rolling across the lake, the wind had tossed and scattered the fallen leaves, yellow and brown and red, which were glued to the soles of their shoes;

the whisky's run out, the driver said; please reconsider, dear sister, the attorney said – but Maura had already taken a step; fine, the solicitor said, fine, let it be as you wish; our driver will pick you up tomorrow morning and we'll all meet at my office in Clifden, the solicitor said; I'll cover the transportation expenses; then we can sign the preliminary contract. Gentlemen, you will be my guests tonight, he said and let out a laugh. And so it was agreed. The men climbed into the car and were soon on their way from the lake to the only town in the area, to Clifden, an hour's drive from here. Maura Ostyn was now, for the first time in a long while, alone again. Although she had remained behind in the middle of a vast, unpopulated and inhospitable landscape, which was slowly disappearing in the long, cold shadows that covered the surface of the silent lake and, with it, the reflection of the manor, the cloudy sky and her own dark silhouette, nevertheless, Jane wrote in her journal, this woman was not entirely alone; the image that had darkened on the water was speaking to her – she would listen to it always, whenever she crouched down by the bed, alone in her narrow room, or, on warm summer nights, when she withdrew from the others and here by the lake, in the shelter of the woods, the stars and the surrounding hills, sought peace; then perhaps, safely concealed by the summer night, Jane wrote, when the manor and the sisters and the girls in the boarding school were sleeping peacefully and the only thing trembling in the night were the tongues of the candles on the water's surface, she would remove her heavy black robe and dip her feet in the cool lake, which is fed by underground pools and mountain torrents, and then dive soundlessly headfirst into the water; she would sink and then motionlessly rise to the surface, Jane wrote. I swam for a long time; in the heated air I heard only the soft splashing of my hands, I didn't come up until I reached the opposite shore, as if night birds were flying through the water, Jane had written; I noticed her long, looping, mysterious handwriting – these sentences have been experienced, have been lived, I thought; this is not a diary or travelogue – Jane was search-ing for something more, I thought when the express train stopped for a moment at the station in Mechelen; through the foggy window I saw women in long overcoats and men in trench coats on the platform; they were holding heavy leather briefcases and large umbrellas with gold clasps; I remembered the woman, my mysterious, nameless narrator; I was listening, she had said; I wasn't sleeping, she had said; from the time I buried my head beneath the pillow, right after hiding my father's sweet gifts, all I did was listen to the words in the darkness, she had said when I came back out to the street holding two glasses of beer; I'm thirsty, I smoke too much, she had said and tasted the foam; Father used to sit in the dark at the kitchen table drinking litre bottles of beer; he would speak clearly and distinctly, even after sitting there a long time by himself; Mama couldn't listen to it any more; she would be crying in the cold hallway, staring at the transom light above the front door; I watched her sometimes, concealing myself at the top of the stairs, the woman had said; she would look at that dark window and flinch every time a light flashed on the glass for even a moment, even if it was just the light of the cold and distant moon, from where nobody could ever be watching us; they're here, they're here, Mama would say, but nobody was ever there, she had said. I've been promoted, Father said in the dark kitchen; they've made me a conductor on the international line; I'll be away for a few days – that's what he always said; my darling, he would cry out in the garden behind our house, where I buried my light-blue box; my darling, he would scream at the moon, they are the same as us, the ones we're taking to Poland, you know, Poland, Auschwitz, my father would be howling, the woman had said; that's what I wanted to tell you, she had said. I'm thirsty; would you mind if we go inside? I'm thirsty, she had said, lighting her last cigarette; she had crumpled the pack and put it in the pocket of her long overcoat. It wasn't until after he died – Marc, I mean – after he'd improvised his life to the end, and our love, too, that I came back to Mechelen; Father hadn't come home after the liberation; he didn't know how to keep secrets, was what Mama said; I knew he wouldn't be able to keep quiet, she said and wrapped herself in her grief. But even so, I later learned that he did come home once, or maybe she had simply told me that; I travel, all I do is travel now by train, first class, Father had said, Mama said; I don't know, the woman had said, by that time she didn't recognize me when I came to see her; dementia, the nurses told me in their grey smocks, and diabetes, a nice young doctor said; it comes with old age, he said; I remember, the woman had said, shaking the ice cubes in her crystal tumbler, I remember Mama lying in bed and looking at the transom light above the door, although by then she was blind; it was the sugar, of course, she had said; it was as if she was still waiting for somebody, the woman had said and sipped her whisky. I moved into the house and lived there by myself; I would go to the nursing home to see her and listen to her, and basically, in the end, Mama would talk just like Father used to, in the dark and to nobody; I think what she said was, you didn't know how to keep secrets, the woman had said; that's all I was able to understand. I paid to have a requiem mass said for her; apparently, this was her last wish – at least, that's what the nurses told me, she had said; I telephoned the canon and we quickly made the arrangements; he didn't ask me anything. We did it on an ordinary weekday, since I didn't want to make a big fuss; it was Mama's wish, after all, not mine, she said; it was at Sint-Pieters-en-Pauluskerk – the Church of Saints Peter and Paul – in Mechelen, which was closest to where I lived; it was completely empty when I went inside, but I knew it right away; it was as if I was that good little girl again, stowing away sweets and family photos in her light-blue box, although, before I went in, I was sure I had never been there before. Slowly, I made my way down the cold, empty nave over the black and white tiles; this is where I was baptized, I was certain of it, she had said, and this is where my aloof father had stood, at the foot of the pulpit, which sits on a large carved wooden globe guarded by snakes and wild animals; I turned when I heard footsteps behind me, echoing through the empty space; this was the very spot my mother had been standing when she held me in her arms, I was certain of it the moment I saw the smiling young priest. We performed the service alone, just the two of us, in silence and dignity; I listened and he read the words out loud, the woman had said. I asked him about it later, when we were standing there alone – what did I have to lose? He said that as far as he was concerned his books were an open record; we went some place in the back and then up a winding staircase; please have a seat, he said; I lit a cigarette; I'll see what I can find, you have my word, Madame, he said kindly, all I need is peace and time. I went home and started digging in the garden; I never did find that beat-up blue box of mine with the six-pointed yellow star on the lid; I know now it's the Star of David, the woman had said, but a few days later I received the original certificate of my baptism in the mail; so it was true, it was all true – that's where I was baptized; I was three years old and it was 1941; my parents were baptized the same day, she had said as I offered her my last cigarette; thanks, she had said, I'll buy some at the station; the train to Mechelen leaves in twenty minutes. Whenever I get off there, or when I'm waiting there for the train, I always think of my father, the loyal, dedicated Belgian Railways conductor; sometimes my Marc will be playing a tune for him on the platform, and, of course, I'm dancing and laughing, still crazy in love; but Mama just sits there by herself on the platform, looking somewhere across the tracks, far away, somewhere she'll never be able to go, the woman had said. I'm Jewish, and if I understood you correctly, that's what you write about, the nameless woman had said, shaking my hand as we said goodbye on the pavement in front of L'Archiduc; it had been raining, just as it was now when the train suddenly started moving again. Next stop: Antwerp, the display said; where Gospođa Spomenka is waiting for me, I thought, as the train sped through Mechelen. I leafed through the journal again and read: I was asking myself, what was Maura looking for, my sister in spirit, on that first night there alone? What had kept her there, what had spoken to her so deeply to make her stay? Jane wrote; was she afraid at first, as I had been? I will never know this, but what I do know is that both she and I had a deep feeling somewhere inside ourselves that we had arrived, we had found our home. Our long search, our wandering, ended here; our journeys and, in a sense, the journeys of all of us converged here, Jane wrote and then went on: In the thick of the night, when the loud autumn wind was blowing across the landscape at full force, a dark and solitary figure, the only living soul within at least an hour's drive, set off bravely into the woods along a muddy, overgrown path to the Gothic chapel, a mere ten minutes' walk from the cold, locked manor. This small-scale replica of a Gothic cathedral was the only thing she had not seen that day; the businessmen with whom she had been rigorously negotiating had not seen the point of showing it to her – it was obvious, more or less, that it came with the property – even if from the very start, when she first heard that incredibly beautiful story, the pure and noble tale of a cathedral in a little grove, standing alone next to the decaying Kylemore Castle, it was the little chapel that had truly attracted her and sent her, not long after, on her unknown journey to this place. She had the feeling that within this story, which had spread persistently by word of mouth, soon becoming a legend more powerful than doubt or discouragement, there was perhaps a hidden message, a clue sent to her by her inner God, by the voice she must have been following ever since that catastrophic move from Ypres; perhaps at that moment, as she stood in front of the heavy doors, the heaviest in her life, Maura thought: the truth is hidden in the journey – long, winding and mysterious are the ways of the Lord. And also this: the homeless, the emigrants, the exiles, all those who eternally roam and wander – these are his first companions. That night for the first time, Maura Ostyn, cold, exhausted and wet, bravely placed her hand on the heavy door handle, Jane wrote, but the doors, as they had been for many years, were securely bolted.

Exactly one month later I took the overnight bus from Ljubljana to Sarajevo, where, after a fairly long period, I again found the peace I needed to write. I arrived there very early in the morning, but only after I had been woken from sleep somewhere near Slavonski Brod and a few moments later was tossed on to the road at a petrol station; the conductor told me his boss had sent them an SMS saying they had to change course – we're going to Banja Luka now, the conductor had said; wait here for the bus from Vienna to Sarajevo; I sent them a message to pick you up, he had said and shut the door. Despite the early hour, my friend Ferida was kind enough to meet me at the Sarajevo bus station; a rosy dawn, I remember, was stretched across the surrounding hills, which were strewn with white minarets and low houses with the blinds drawn; the traffic was just beginning to stir; in the green tram in front of us, a young woman in a white jacket sat by the window combing her long auburn hair; you'll have peace to write here, I'm glad you came, Ferida said as we drove to my temporary accommodation on Josip Vančas Street, a stone's throw from the centre of town. In the mornings, I usually sat on the balcony, which had a view of the courtyard, reading and watching the children and their mischievous dogs playing and running on the soft grass; their grandmothers in long skirts would come and sit on the benches beneath a tall spruce tree and chat over coffee, while the young mothers would be hanging laundry on the balconies or, even at that early hour, cooking – the courtyard would fill with the aroma of fresh dough and roasted meat each time one of the housewives in their colourful blouses opened her warm kitchen and came out for a cigarette or to check on the children; I heard them calling their names; I remember they always made some friendly comment whenever a dog started barking too loudly below. Men and husbands were absent, I noticed, as if they were all away on business, or they wouldn't come home from work until late in the evening; only rarely did I see a shape appear on the balcony after a late supper, smoking a cigarette and drinking a beer; I had the impression, as I watched them from my dark balcony, that they were looking somewhere across the rooftops, past the chimneys, to a hill where you could hear the rustle of broadleafs and conifers; they stood there motionless, slowly smoking their cigarettes; something inside them was still smouldering, a fire still glowing that had been extinguished hastily and of necessity, but that could at any moment explode, like a cold, dark, distant star, I thought.

I took two short trips out of the city, I remember, to Mostar and
Travnik; Senadin drove me; we had met earlier in Ljubljana – I think
it was at a supper after a lecture he had given. In Travnik, I visited the
house where Andrić was born, then Senadin and I climbed the hill
to the former mighty fortress of the viziers, which still stands defiant
above the town; it was a cloudy day; a curtain of fog reached down to
the minarets and the tall, well-bolted houses; the buildings still bore
deep, gaping holes on their façades and rooftops, like open wounds
from the last war. We sat down in a garden by a murmuring mountain
stream, where we were served Turkish coffee, a small piece of sweet
pastry and cigarettes; I remember the silence, the reserve and inner
tension that pervaded the city, as if somewhere in the background
somebody was intoning a gruesome narrative, which was obscured by
the sound of living water falling and flowing beneath the rocks, living
water that was gushing from the open wounds. The body of the earth is
bleeding, I thought, or maybe this is new life, water bathing wounded
bodies, washing away tears, I said; the men were sitting in silence, and

now, as I write this, I think they must still be sitting at those tables, slowly pouring coffee into tiny cups from the *džezva*; across the street, women in black niqabs were leaning against a wall; the silence and the murmur of the stream were drowned out by the muezzin's voice from the loudspeakers on the minarets; there is a kind of difference, Senadin said, that maybe is even deeper than ontological difference – I'm writing about it in my new book, he said; as a philosopher, I'm curious about how we think the body today, and what's more, how does the body think, how do we approach the world through the body, beyond words? he said and smiled; on the narrow road in front of the garden two big tourist buses met head to head; nobody will leave here unharmed, he said; we watched the bored and weary passengers leap off the buses and start running to the coffee house, but there were only a few tables, all occupied, and unfortunately, only a single hole in the lavatory, somewhere behind the building; I remember there was a long queue in front of it. The women in black left quickly and shut themselves in their houses, while the men turned away from the road and immersed themselves in their heavy thoughts as they slowly smoked their cigarettes. To put it in radical terms, Senadin said, I am seeking a language that speaks of the absent body, he said; psychoanalysis, of course, has opened the body for us, but there is a terrifying abyss beneath it, the terrifying kingdom of dreams, Senadin said; Lacan was absolutely right when he said that the unconscious is structured like language, which means that the body, which tells a story, is alive, seeks its desire, seeks heaven, which, however, is for ever hidden from it, like the dead letter on paper, Senadin said; but, he said, think of language, of living poetic speech, which is able again and again to discover, address and inhabit its own absent dead body, he said; I write about this in my book *The Heavenly Shovel*, about the heaven that we soldiers bury in the ground every day, preferably very early in the morning before we've spoken our last desire. This is the language of sweet plums, ripe and juicy, which hang above your lost body at arm's reach, so to speak, calling to you in their heavenly language, but you know that the moment you lift your head or raise your arm, you'll be mowed down by machine-gun fire.

From time to time, Senadin would drive his wife – who on our trip sat in the back seat watching the baby – to her classes in Mostar; on one of these occasions they were kind enough to take me with them. We drove slowly across the hills and plateaus, climbing a narrow, winding road; there was still snow on the high, steep peaks, but in the valley the meadows were already completely green, the trees rich in blossoms, and children in T-shirts sat by the road selling spring flowers, honey and brandy; this is the same road I took during the war, twice, when I managed to leave Sarajevo just so I could get some air, Ita said; we only travelled at night, on a little beat-up bus, and as soon as we left the city the driver switched off all the lights, she said; we didn't say a word the entire trip; I closed my eyes but I couldn't sleep – I was driving in my mind, Ita said, as if blindfolded, weaving along the dark snowy road and praying, although I didn't know the right words, that we wouldn't skid off a cliff or be spotted by soldiers or stopped by bandits; we knew that everyone must certainly be able to see us from a distance, she said, and could easily start shooting at us, Ita said and caressed the baby; as soon as light appeared on the horizon, I remember, the driver tried to get us – before the bleak and lifeless landscape had extracted itself from the false security of the night – to the foot of the highest mountain pass, she said, and then he quickly turned off the road and parked somewhere in the woods; right away, we all ran off in different directions, deep into the surrounding area; then we wrapped ourselves in blankets and white sheets and hid behind the rocks or in the few bushes there were, and some of us took shelter in the ruins of the burned-out houses, Ita said; we didn't dare light a fire; we just sat there in silence, cold and frightened, she said; I knew I would be an easy target out in the open; I didn't move an inch until it was night, but when night fell and all you could see were the cold, hazy outlines of the world, we pushed the bus back on the road and continued our journey through the mountains in the dark, Ita said.

Look, said Senadin, the Neretva River, see how clean and green it is. We were going down hairpin bends into a deep ravine, as the light broke against the sharp, precipitous walls that fell into the river, I remember; we stopped at an inn along the road; the warm morning sun had just emerged above the gorge and was shining on the Neretva; in the flashing of the water and in the fresh air that had drifted down along the river from the mountains and was soon mixed with the wind that must have risen somewhere far away over the Adriatic, I thought, it suddenly struck me, as if a strong, deep image from my memory had surprised and taken hold of me: *déjà vu*, I thought, or perhaps there really was a sudden smell of the sea in the air, as in a beautiful distant memory, I thought; we used to stop here, I'm sure of it, when my parents and I would be driving to the seaside, I said. The baby had fallen asleep in Ita's lap and Senadin put her in the child seat, strapping her in with the safety belt. Back during the war it would take us two or three days to get to Mostar by bus; I don't know why but it was usually faster coming back; it was like getting caught in a mousetrap again and again, she said; you hop in and then you can't get out, Ita said; people sometimes got stuck here for a week at a time when there was too much shooting going on, the driver told me, Ita said, if they didn't get killed first, of course, or locked up in a camp, or at least chased back home, Ita said as we drove along the long, straight road to Mostar; the valley had opened out and now there were only stony hills rising gently in the distance; the air shimmered with an early summer haze, and far ahead of us the road disappeared into the sea – a mirage, I realized; Senadin stopped the car at a roadside stand and bought a bag of the season's first small red cherries, which would soon reach the Sarajevo market, too, I remember; the apricots aren't ready yet, he

said and drove on to the Faculty of Humanities, in a Mostar suburb, where his wife, Ita, teaches 'Introduction to Aesthetics'.

Today Mostar is a totally divided city, Senadin said and rolled up his sleeves; he was pushing the stroller slowly; the baby was asleep; the three of us had gone for a walk while Ita taught her class. You see? This side is exclusively Croat; they have locked themselves away, fenced themselves off, on their own side of the street; that new church of theirs, which they say has the highest tower in the region, Senadin said, although it mostly looks like a local fire station, he said, this piece of soulless architecture – it's their rediscovered identity now, he said; we crossed the busy boulevard and went down to the river; the sound of the living water as it tumbled over the gleaming white stones was mixed with the voices of tourists, sacramental song and the cries of street vendors; it's always like this, he said, it's always full of people, too many people, Senadin said; we picked up the stroller and pushed our way across the new stone bridge to the opposite bank of the Neretva.

This is all that's left to the Bosniaks now, a few narrow old streets and that steep hillside up there, he said, pointing at the new houses that stood scattered among the scree in the baking sun, without trees or grass; the stone they used for replicating the old bridge will be worn down and burnished to a shine before anybody other than Japanese tourists with their cameras or officials from international NGOs walks across it, Senadin said, centuries will have to go by, and a lot of southern wind and summer heat, before people on both sides of the river again find the courage to drink together from the Neretva, Senadin said and unfolded a blanket in the soft shade by the water, lifted the baby from the stroller, cradled her in his arms, and then laid her on the soft blanket; in the distance, the slender stone arc curved over the river, as if hovering in the quivering air between the sky and the earth; Senadin and I rolled up our trouser legs and stepped barefoot into the icy river, to cool our burning feet; in fact, this is just a clean, green river that happens to flow beneath a bridge on its way to the sea, Senadin said. The little girl had woken up and was waving her tiny arms, disturbed by bits of sunlight dancing in the treetops; she wants to catch them in her hand, I thought; I don't believe he's really going to dive, Senadin said, wading deeper into the water; look, he said; a diver was standing on the edge of the stone bridge with his arms spread out; it's just a paid performance for the foreign tourists, he said; the boys who used to swan-dive there for nothing are long dead, he said. The diver slowly lowered his arms and held them close to his body, then elegantly leaned forward, swaying back and forth above the cool, clean, green river, which far below was flowing to the sea. Perfect symmetry.

I was reading the short story collections *Turkish Tales* and *Sea Tales*, by Ivo Andrić, this time in the original Serbian; I had also brought with me a big illustrated book about Sarajevo and a photocopy of Andrić's *Letter from 1920*, which Spomenka had talked to me about in Antwerp; my friend Tone, in Ljubljana, had lent me the books. My afternoons were

spent in long walks; I went all over the city and visited the locations and routes Spomenka had described to me, or sometimes in the morning I would go to the market, buy a full bag of the first Mostar cherries, a tomato and fresh bread; then I'd go down to the Miljacka River, where I'd have a coffee, walk slowly back to the flat and spend the whole day writing these lines. One Friday morning, after we had coffee at the Buybook bookshop, my friend Ahmed walked me to a cab in front of the Skenderija centre; I remember how we had met years earlier at the airport in Sarajevo. It wasn't long after the war, and regular flights from Ljubljana had just started up again; outside it was already night, and I remember that it was raining heavily and in front of the entrance, where Ahmed was waiting for us with a big smile, there were large patches of muddy snow left over from a recent blizzard; I had flown there with a group of friends – Tina, Špela, Miran, Mitja, Marko and Esad, if I remember correctly – and as soon as I stepped out of the musty terminal into the night air, I gathered up some wet, heavy, muddy snow and squeezed it into a big hard ball, I remember, and threw it at Ahmed, who was giving us all hugs; it struck his cap, which fell into the mud; he had smiled and hugged me, although I knew it must have hurt; you're my friend, he had said; we'll get along, he had said. Later he had told me he had returned home just a few months before; he had been in Ljubljana during the war; I stayed here as long as I could; I left Sarajevo when I ran out of words, he had said; now I'm learning my mother tongue all over again; I want people here to understand each other again, one day I'd like to write a poem about it, he had said as we drove slowly to the city; for a long time now, I've been diligently learning my mother tongue, it's been fifteen years, Ahmed said as we walked to the Skenderija; I think I finally managed to write that poem, but my mother still doesn't understand it, he said; she will never understand me, Ahmed said; I gave him a hug and climbed in the cab, which had been waiting for me. I went to the Kovačići neighbourhood and, in peace and quiet, looked at the Jewish cemetery, which has stood on a hill above Sarajevo for five hundred years. I strolled for a long time among the white gravestones,

which lay in the tall spring grass; it was not until the afternoon, when the shadows were already descending on the city below, that I went back down the hill on foot to the centre of town; I was thinking about Spomenka and the long story she had told me. This is the only image I have retained – the view of the courtyard from my old flat in Sarajevo, Gospoda Spomenka had said; I often catch myself thinking I'm still there on those mornings when I take the train to Ghent and I'm tired and sleepy; that's when I see again the long shadows falling on the city from the surrounding hills, when the sun has just risen above the minarets and church towers, the shadows that would then lie hidden for a long time in the narrow streets, she had said; I would watch them from the balcony in my bathrobe, with a cigarette and a cup of coffee in my hand; it's strange the way everything else has been burned away by the distance, by the miles of train tracks that divide us, my relatives, my friends and acquaintances, and nothing remains but trivial details, which at times can suddenly float to the surface, unexpectedly and painlessly, like a play of light and shadow, Gospoda Spomenka had said to me when we saw each other again at the train station in Antwerp, just a few days after our first meeting. She was waiting for me in front of the entrance; I arrived at exactly ten thirty-five, having left Brussels at ten o'clock after quick goodbyes with Gjini on the platform; we had arranged to meet at eleven, so there was still time for me to have a quick look round the station, which was once considered a true cathedral of the railways, as Sebald writes in his superb novel *Austerlitz*. I slowly ascended the escalator from the underground platforms, built just a few years earlier, to the first level, where the trains once stopped, which was covered by a monumental semicircular construction of iron and glass; I later read online that the renovation and modernization of this railway cathedral had been entrusted to the architect Jacques Voncke, who was also responsible for the extensive renovation of the train station in Ghent, where Gjini had forgotten his journal, which I had been reading on the train trip here; now as I was looking around this magnificent example of railway architecture, I still held it in my hands. I had a few more minutes;

outside it was starting to rain and there were thick grey clouds lying over the city, as I saw through the high windows; I entered the café, where in former times, beneath the big station clock and heavy crystal chandeliers, only first-class passengers would have been sitting, over coffee and warm soup, with newspapers in their hands; this is where they waited for their trains and were in no hurry to be anywhere, I thought. It was unusually quiet and calm; even the hands on the big clock were standing still; everyone had departed. I ordered coffee and flipped through a few more pages of the journal; I was trying to find an entry that would tell me if Jane had been in Antwerp; I turned the pages quickly, checking to see if the city's name jumped out at me anywhere; she had definitely been to Mechelen, only half an hour away, so she had very likely come to Antwerp, too, and maybe even sat for a while in this quiet train station café, I thought, but right then I wasn't able to find anything she wrote that would confirm this; later, in the evening, however, on the train back to Brussels, from where I would be leaving the next day early in the morning for Charleroi, where I would visit the Photography Museum and in the afternoon fly to Trieste, then go home by road – on the train ride from Antwerp, then, I finally found a few words, a hint, that Jane had, in fact, been there. The sentence was on the page that directly followed her long and anguished description of the museum in Mechelen: I am so shaken by what I saw here that I can't think any more about their cut diamonds, which I had planned to see this afternoon; the only thing I want to look at is the open sea; I'll go all the way out to the port and try to breathe again, Jane had written.

I remember that big chipped teacup with Vučko, the Olympic mascot, on it, which my husband had given me during the Sarajevo Olympics; if I'm not mistaken, it was a Slovene who created him; we all knew his name back then, Gospođa Spomenka said; yes, I said, Jože Trobec, the Slovene artist who drew the mascot, I said; I know his daughter Špela; she's a painter, too; we even used to share a studio, but she's been living in Spain the past few years, somewhere on the Atlantic coast, I said; well, it's a little country – you all know each other

there, Gospođa Spomenka said as we walked slowly down the wide street from Antwerp train station to the centre of town, without any plan or goal; it was drizzling and the big city appeared empty to me; see over there? all those places are Jewish diamond dealers, she said. I never imagined they would be the ones – I mean the Sarajevo Jews, of course – who would

Sarajevo '84

one day save our lives; I guess you never know, she said and stopped at the corner; we turned off the main road and the streets became narrower and narrower; leaning against a building, she shielded her lighter with her coat so the cold wind that had risen over the Scheldt River, which was hidden in the background behind some buildings, would not rob her of the flame. As she smoked, she pointed at a tall church tower that curved into the grey sky at the end of the street; that's the Cathedral of Our Lady; there are lots of nice pubs in the area – I'm cold and it's almost noon, so let's get warm, she said; I've taken the day off. As part of my opening lecture I usually read my students Andrić's famous *Letter from 1920*, Gospođa Spomenka said; we were sitting in a little pub near Groenplaats with two empty glasses in front of us on a long wooden table; I've had enough of your *Gospođa* – I'm Spomenka, just call me Spomenka; after all, we're both from the same part of the world, she said when our silent waiter had again filled our glasses right to the brim; go on, drink up, Spomenka said and bent over her glass to sip the strong drink from the edge so it wouldn't spill. It always reminds me of home; it's the only thing you can get here that at least resembles our liquor; I've been coming to this pub ever since I moved to Antwerp, usually alone; my Belgian guy doesn't drink spirits, just beer, she said; I used to drink this when I was writing letters and postcards so I wouldn't start crying, although I had no idea if the Sarajevo postmen would still be able to find the right address, since you know, she said and tapped her empty glass against the wood, these new Muslims, who were all suddenly reborn after the war, they changed all the names – on the houses, the streets,

even on the graves, she said; I have the feeling that the young Muslims today must outnumber even the green leaves on the chestnuts beside my lazy Miljacka, Spomenka said; it was there beneath the chestnut trees that my dear Andrić used to walk at night by the river with his melancholy young friend Max Levenfeld, who, although he was baptized, was still a Jew by birth – our only Nobel laureate writes about it in his *Letter*, Spomenka said. You know, I went back a few years ago – it had been many years since we left Sarajevo, my daughter Zora and me, Spomenka said; we didn't escape, I'm not a refugee! – that's what Zora always told her Belgian schoolmates – well, on that brief visit, our first short holiday in Sarajevo, Spomenka said, I could barely recognize the city; the streets had been entirely relabelled and renamed; the old red number plates on the buildings, which once bore the names of our national heroes and great Yugoslav writers, had been replaced by big green signs shining with names I didn't know – various Suleimans, Ali Pashas, Hajjis and long-extinct Beys, she said; my old neighbours, people who used to drink raki and listen to music with

us in our flat, were suddenly wrapped in long black robes; old friends of mine, women who in the past, when we were still alive, used to parade around the city in miniskirts and sunbathe next to the Miljacka in bikinis – I remember how on Sundays we'd get together and hang out with the boys by the Eternal Flame on Marshal Tito Street, then stroll through the Old Bazaar with our ice cream, and on those late summer evenings, when the humidity in the air refused to evaporate from the sweltering Sarajevo Valley and would roll through the streets all the way to dawn, through the churches and prayer halls, the bustling open-air restaurants, the cafés and sports arenas where you could hear Yugo rock playing, we would sit on the fountains far into the night – *česme* we called them – drinking the cold water that poured from the walls around the Bey Mosque, Spomenka said and concealed her empty glass in her palm; we were all trying to cool off and would mix that water with Macedonian wine – *vranec* I think it was, she said; well, today these same women would rather cover their faces than wear makeup – I don't know what they're ashamed of, Spomenka said. Our old boyfriends and boring husbands, the blokes we played the

love game with, who used to recite poems by Sidran in a single voice and were always quoting Kusturica's films – they're to blame for everything, she said; they thought they had grown up overnight, that they understood the world, the complex questions of nationality, and suddenly modern literature wasn't enough for them any more; just like that, while we women were suffering the pains of childbirth and growing old, they switched to ethno music and started believing passionately in long-forgotten myths and epics and legends; it's horrible, she said; there's nothing there that's beautiful and happy any more, Spomenka said. I'm telling you, when we left, the city lost its soul; not even the water is as clear and cool as it used to be, she said and got up from the table, went over to the waiter, and set her glass on the bar; wordlessly he filled it to the brim without spilling a drop. I'm going outside for a cigarette; do you smoke? she said; yes, I said, surprised she hadn't noticed. It was cold on the damp asphalt pavement; we stood in front of the empty pub, the waiter eyeing us silently through the window; we each lit a second cigarette. I'm talking too much,

I know; I should make my story, my confession, shorter; I remember a few strange and, at least for me, incomprehensible demonstrations in front of the Presidency Building; all at once, for the first time in a long time, everyone was out on the streets; everyone had their own demands, but together we were all demanding some sort of lasting peace; it was strange, she said; a few days later my former husband stopped coming home from his regular coffee house; he left me alone with the child; then the tram stopped running, and they cut off our water and electricity, so it was impossible to keep working and teaching at the university, she said. Then one evening – it was autumn, but it was still warm and there was the smell of leaves and fire in the air; it got into our homes and into our clothes, I remember, I couldn't get rid of it, this invasive, strange, yet also pleasant smell, the smell of pine trees – well, she said, that was the last time I saw him – my ex-husband, I mean; he showed up a little after eleven and stayed almost till morning. The moment he stepped through the door – he still had his key; he hadn't lost it the entire year he'd been gone, although in the past he would usually have to change the lock a few times a year because he'd forget his coat at the coffee house and leave the keys in the pocket; he was a journalist, Spomenka said, and he always said the coffee house was where he did his work; sure it is, I'd say to myself; somebody took my coat by mistake, or maybe stole it – that was all my dear husband would say, and then he'd ring up our neighbour, a carpenter, and ask him to change the lock. Well, he hadn't lost his key this time; he quietly unlocked the door – I still removed the key from the lock the way I used to do so he could sneak in from the coffee house and come to me – well, the moment he walked through the door I knew it was him even in the dark; he smelled of pine trees; I hadn't gone to bed yet; I was sitting by the window holding my big little girl in my arms; I remember I was reading Andrić's fairy-tale *Aska and the Wolf* to her; actually, I knew it by heart, Spomenka said; well, that little girl of mine – she's done very well for herself, of course, and is rich, too; she's a top manager in a multinational, she said – well, now she doesn't want to hear a thing about fairy tales, and what's worse, as soon as we arrived here she said she never wanted to hear her mother tongue again: *Mother, speak proper language*, Zora told me; as for me, I needed a few years to learn the language and get my qualification to teach at university, Spomenka said, but kids forget things fast and learn even faster, she said. That's just how it goes, but it's the one thing that really hurts – there's nobody I can talk to in my own language any more; all I have left are my students, and they will never understand me, she said. Come on, let's sit a little and get warm, she said. We went back inside the empty pub; our glasses were still on the table; the waiter arrived with the bottle and Spomenka pointed to me; I nodded and the waiter adroitly filled the glass to the brim; he then turned with the bottle to Spomenka and was about to pour, but she quickly covered her glass with her hand and looked away, somewhere outside.

It was the last time we lay together as a couple, right after he came up to me without saying a word and I put the child down on the sofa and opened the window as far as it would go – I guess I couldn't stand that smell any more, it was like he had brought all the scorched trees, the charred forests, into the flat with him – shut the window this minute, my husband said, and close the curtains, he said, our men are watching us from the hill, the snipers see everything, he said, Spomenka said; I watch you sometimes with binoculars in the evening; I'm looking out for you two; I'm not far away, just up in Kovačići, by the old Jewish cemetery – that's where I have my office, my husband said and ripped off the only decent dress I still had. I took off his damp army coat; he was still wearing that warm, comfortable sweatsuit, the one he used to wear on Sundays when he'd stretch out on the sofa, where my Zora was lying now, and watch football; he always rooted for Red Star Belgrade. It was like a scorched tree had fallen on top of me, tall, heavy and rough; I was gasping for air, my mouth was full of sap; it was like branches were breaking deep inside me, shedding their dry needles; my arms were wrapped around sharp pine bark, which was scratching and hurting me; I was climbing up the trunk so I wouldn't sink into the ground, Spomenka said and ordered a glass of beer. I didn't have the strength any more to keep lugging two buckets of water a day up to the seventh floor; I knew winter was coming soon, the second winter Zora and I would have to wait for alone. At the first snow, which started coming down slowly in the afternoon and kept getting heavier throughout the night – it was just before Christmas – so that when we woke up in the morning there was a peculiar silence, a kind of peace, and for a moment I felt like a burden had been lifted from everyone in the city, as if the snow had covered up all the living and the dead, the men on the hill who were watching us and us below, who were waiting for them to descend into the city, to come home, oh, I don't know, she said; let's take a winter holiday and just stay there, Zora said to me that morning out of the blue; I was gathering up snow from the balcony so I could brew the pinch of camomile I'd received from my neighbour, the carpenter; he had told me I should go to the Bonavalencia office, their pharmacy and humanitarian agency, or I could just stop by the old Sephardic Synagogue if I needed anything, my carpenter neighbour had said, Spomenka said; thank you, neighbour, I said, and only later did it hit me: my friendly, smiling neighbour, the good carpenter, our own Mišo, who had so often changed our lock for free, he was an old Sarajevo Jew – who'd have imagined it? Spomenka said; I never knew that before. Mišo the carpenter, too, had never asked who, or what, I was, not even now, Spomenka said and took a big draught of the cold beer. So as I was saying, she said, it was just before the Catholic Christmas (we have ours a little later) and I pulled on my old filthy coat and tied a big woollen scarf around my head to hide my face, although I don't know why – it was instinctive – and took a wicker basket from the cupboard, one that in better times I used to take to the market on Saturdays, and said to Zora, I'm going shopping, Spomenka said, and for the first time in a long while we both smiled. Outside, you could hear popping noises in the distance, but I thought it was the trees snapping from the cold, somewhere in the mountains, on Jahorina or Bjelašnica, since there were almost no trees left in the city – the ones around the apartment blocks had all been cut down for firewood, she said; I was plodding through the deep untrodden snow, even though it was almost nine and people in those days did all their chores early in the morning, even before the sun came up, and then we'd just sit in the dark hallways or lie in our cold beds, she said, but that day everything seemed beautiful and simple to me again; the white sun was shining on the white city; I was even peeking into the broken and looted shop windows, just to pass the time, and amusing myself with my memories, which were themselves becoming more broken and more looted every day; I'm not sure but I think somebody was even burning rubbish that day in front of the Eternal Flame, which had gone out long ago, she said. I went into the chilly City Market and for a second broke into a sweat, even though it was icy as a tomb; the concrete tables were covered in debris, and a few shivering orphans with tear-stained faces were hiding there, as well as younger children wrapped in coarse blankets; there was nothing there for Christmas, neither theirs nor ours, I thought; I ran outside; the snow was still pristine; far and wide, along the long road

through the city, and perhaps even further out, across the hills and valleys, and on towards the sea, I thought, there was nothing but my own tiny, crooked trail winding through the snow; I headed for the Old Bazaar; there was no one playing chess in front of our church that morning, just headless figures sticking out of the snow; I recognized a black king and a white queen; then there was another pop, I remember, and another one, louder this time; I knew it wasn't the trees, Jahorina was too far away; I heard glass breaking, the machine-gun fire was somewhere high above my scarfed head. I didn't run, I plodded my way in between two buildings and in their shelter lit a half-cigarette; so that's how our men watch over the city, I thought, they shoot at their own women, Spomenka said. I was running out of everything – tobacco, will, food – there were moments I felt like I was running out of love, too, Spomenka said. I turned my glass over; I felt a chill. I had never asked anybody for anything; somehow we had always managed to get by, one way or another, she said; I pulled the scarf off my head and draped it around my shoulders; I combed my hair with my frozen fingers and rubbed new-fallen snow on my cheeks, Spomenka said and ran her hand through her hair; it was the first time I had ever really been inside the old Synagogue – I had had no reason to before; I had seen it from the outside and that was enough for me, she said; I remember a lamp with a candle was hanging on a long chain and its flame flickered when I entered; there were people sitting on the floor, sorting papers, filling boxes, counting coats and shirts; I said, in a casual sort of way, that I was here to see my neighbour Mišo, my neighbour the carpenter, she said; certainly, madam, welcome, shalom, a man with large eyeglasses said, wait here, please. Spomenka finished off her beer; somebody came into the pub; she grabbed her books and notebook, which earlier, when she was looking for her cigarettes, she had placed on the table. Let's get out of here; I told my Belgian guy that I'd heat up half a chicken for him and bring home some *pommes frites* from town; he loves his chicken and chips, she said; he'll be home at four. Let's go, Spomenka said; I'll treat you to some *pommes frites*, the real thing – they do excellent ones on Groenplaats. I paid for the drinks and we left.

We were standing in the wind holding big greasy paper bags of chips in our hands; shoo! shoo! Spomenka said, flapping her arms; I'm afraid of pigeons, I'm afraid they'll carry off my soul, she said and shielded her cheeks from the flock of grey pigeons that flew up off the paved square. They smelled the hot chips, she said; sometimes I think they recognize me, that they've come here straight from

Sarajevo – there they're everywhere, it's horrible; that's another reason I don't want to go back again, Spomenka said. OK, let me finish my story, she said, I had just lit the half-cigarette in peace when my dear neighbour, Mišo the carpenter, appears from somewhere covered in dust; please forgive me, Mišo said and wiped his hands on his trousers, ever since morning I've been sawing wood for coffins – it's been a bloody Saturday, Mišo said and smiled; no, no, I said, Zora and I would like to take a winter holiday, I said, Spomenka said; shoo, shoo! get the hell away! she said and stamped her foot on the pavement, goddamn pigeons. I couldn't think of anything else, she said, that's all I said to our neighbour; we had never really had a conversation before but, surprisingly, he understood me; I think he's the only person who ever understood what I was saying, Spomenka said.

I don't know if it was meant as a gift or if it was merely coincidence, but the day before our Orthodox Christmas I found a note in front of my door written in thick carpenter's pencil on crêpe paper. I still have it today; it's stored away somewhere in one of the books I managed to take with me when I left, Spomenka said.

It didn't take more than a few days for me to forget all about the visit to the synagogue; it was out of my thoughts the moment Zora and I finished the dry bread and tin of fish paste – everything Mišo had packed up for me; we had nothing left but a few camomile teabags, which we had been saving for Christmas but had to use the week before, on New Year's Eve, because we were so cold; we were both in bed with a fever. I read the note again, this time out loud; Zora, who was still unwell and lying on the sofa, listened to me in amazement: *Tomorrow at 3pm be packed and ready, I'm taking you out of town. We're going on a winter holiday, a long trip. Leave your keys with me! Your neighbour, Mišo.* I knew what this meant; even Zora guessed it right away – she was shouting and jumping up and down on our old sofa like she'd gone insane; *Mama, let's go! Let's go crazy!* Zora said in English, Spomenka said. My darling daughter, tomorrow is Christmas and you and I are going on a winter holiday, a long one, maybe for good, I said; *yes!* Zora said. We packed two suitcases with warm clothes, took a few photos out of the family album, and I selected some books from my depleted shelves, mainly ones that were thin and light – a lot of them I had burned to keep us warm and a few others I'd exchanged for winter shoes for Zora, whose feet were still growing, war or no war, Spomenka said. I went into the bathroom, opened the cabinet and took out the box where I used to keep my jewellery; the only piece I had left was a diamond ring, an heirloom, a gift from my mother, in fact; I had hidden it long before, I'm not sure why, buried it in some old yellowed Solea hand cream, she said; I dipped my finger in the cream, which smelled the way it always had, dug out the ring and wiped it on my dry, cracked palms; then I quickly stuck it in my bra, where I still carry it today, she said; you never know when you might get lost in the snow, she said; I can always sell it to the Jews who deal in diamonds here, she said. My hands were greasy and fragrant from that old cream for quite some time, she said. Wash yourself off with snow, I told Zora, and I'll put some cream on you; tomorrow is Christmas and we are going on a trip; we need to be clean and tidy, I told Zora. Zora didn't want to take anything with her from her room, not books, not toys; I'll be studying, Zora said, at my new school I'm going to study hard all the time, I'll be the best student in the class; no one will criticize me any more for not being one of them, you'll see, she said, Spomenka said. Then we went to bed and tried to fall asleep – just to make the time go faster and so we'd forget about being cold and hungry, Spomenka said. I heard there's a wonderful zoo in Antwerp, right behind the train station; that will be the first place we go to when we get there, I told Zora; we couldn't sleep, we just lay there with our eyes closed, buried under the damp blankets; we're going to Belgium, our neighbour Mišo will arrange everything with his friends, I said, Spomenka said. That was the longest day of my life, Spomenka said; I was a child again, younger than my own daughter, she said; I was afraid, but I was also excited about the trip, the way I used to be when my parents would take me on trips to Jahorina, or Mostar, or even to the sea, to Makarska and Dubrovnik – I remember telling that to Zora, Spomenka said. Do they have a white tiger there?

Zora asked; where? I said; in Antwerp, Zora said; I don't know, I said; what do you mean you don't know? Zora said; so why are we going there then? Zora said; I don't know, I said, I don't know, don't ask me; if you want, I'll talk to the man at the gate and ask him to let us in the zoo, since I don't have any Belgian money, and then we can see for ourselves if there's a white tiger living there, I said, Spomenka said. In Sarajevo a white tiger would get lost for sure, Zora said; now why's that? I said, when it was already getting light outside; I was scared of what Zora might be thinking; why do you think it would get lost? are you afraid Daddy might shoot it from the hill? I asked cautiously; oh no, Zora said; the white tiger would get lost in the white snow – everything is white outside, Zora said when that afternoon someone knocked politely on our door, Spomenka said. We stood up; we were already in our shoes and coats; we had made the bed, straightened the curtains and put away the cups, she said; the one with Vučko I was leaving behind on purpose; it will be here waiting for me, I thought, Spomenka said.

You can leave the keys with me, Mišo said when I had turned the key twice in the door and both Zora and I had twice checked the handle to make sure we had locked it securely. I took the key from the keyhole and placed it in his hand; don't worry, I know how to look after keys; I still have a big old key from Spain in a drawer at home, from when we had to leave there in the Middle Ages, just like the two of you, unfortunately, have to go away now, he said, but don't worry, your key will be waiting for you when you come back, Mišo said. Let's go, they're waiting for us, he said, Spomenka said. We went down the dark stairwell to the ground floor, and I never went up those stairs again, Spomenka said, but there's a light burning again in our flat, I saw it from a distance years later, when I was there on a short holiday; I never asked who turned it on, I don't want to know who has the keys, she said.

We were waiting for the tram, having first stopped at a shop where Spomenka bought half a chicken in cling film; she was going to heat it in the microwave, she said; she'd already bought the chips; her Belgian

guy loved this, she said; they'd have a big bottle of beer with it; he never drinks hard liquor, just beer, she said; I'm full, she said, so I won't be eating. We boarded the tram and set off towards the train station; I'm getting off two stops ahead of you; I need to change trams, she said and took an empty seat; I sat down on the narrow seat in front of her. The rain was coming down slowly, just a drizzle, as if a light translucent cloud had settled on the city. The bell rang and the tram rumbled forward.

There was a white Volkswagen Golf standing in the deep snow in front of the building; look, Mama, a white tiger, Zora said, Spomenka said; she was talking to me from behind my back, loudly, but nobody on the tram could understand her and nobody was looking at us. We drove along a snow-covered road through Marin Dvor, past the Skenderija, and then suddenly uphill; we're going to the old Jewish cemetery in Kovačići, Mišo said, Spomenka said; nobody said anything after that; you couldn't see anything through the misted windows, and it was dark outside; the car was driving without lights,

Spomenka said. We went as far as we could, but the Golf got stuck in the snow on a steep incline. You'll have to walk from here, the driver said; Mišo pressed a dollar note in his hand but I don't know how much it was; I didn't have any money myself, she said; we got out and the car drove back down in reverse. Everything was quiet, I remember; the dark city below us was already wrapped in the evening fog, Spomenka said. Mišo was carrying our suitcases and Zora and I held hands and trudged up the hill. At the cemetery gate a man welcomed us and led us to the chapel; wait here, he said and shut the door; it felt like we were being shut inside a tomb. I could sense that we weren't alone, but nobody was talking or crying; all you could hear in that icy chamber was breathing, Spomenka said. For a second I let go of Zora's hand and then thought I would never find her again in the darkness. Zora! Zora! I cried, Spomenka said; be quiet, somebody said, and then added: be quiet, we're listening. And then I heard the singing; I don't know, maybe I was the only one who heard it; when I found Zora's hand again and squeezed it tight, I heard my daughter singing an old Christmas carol; that was the last time I heard her sing in our language, she said, or maybe the song was, in fact, coming from somewhere far away, from the top of the hill, I don't know, she said. Then the heavy door opened into the night. Mišo handed us our suitcases and wished us a wonderful winter holiday. Keep going slowly to the top of the cemetery – that's where your people are waiting for you, they're celebrating Christmas; everything's been arranged, my neighbour Mišo said and went back into the chapel; I heard the lock click. I knew we were being watched, but I didn't see anybody; the soldiers were lying in the deep snow, hidden behind the old gravestones. We made our way slowly through the snow; I was too afraid to even look back. Our trail was covered quickly by the falling snow; it had been snowing since morning, Spomenka said; the carol soon died down, or maybe I was the only one who heard it, she said. I felt nothing but rough hands, saw only shadows, greeting us at the top. I asked where the office was, and the shadows broke into laughter; my husband's a journalist, he works here, I said, Spomenka said; Zora and I are going on holiday; I haven't seen or heard from my husband for months and my daughter would like to say goodbye to her father, I said; well, lady, somebody said out of the dark; your husband has probably left the country, he's a foreign correspondent now; he'll get in touch with you someday, he said, Spomenka said.

The tram came to a stop; just one more stop and after that I get off, she said. We didn't wake up until we reached the train station in Slavonski Brod; the whole bus trip – the bus had been waiting for us at the top of the cemetery – we slept as if drugged. It won't be long now, my little one, I said to Zora, and maybe you will see that white tiger at the Antwerp zoo, I said when we were safely at the station, Spomenka said. Only much later, when I was already teaching our literature in Ghent, did I realize the full greatness, and also the irony, of great literature; I always remember the scene in Andrić's *Letter from 1920* – he, too, said goodbye for ever to his young friend Max Levenfeld at the train station in Slavonski Brod; they were both leaving Sarajevo. Max, a disillusioned demobbed soldier from the battlefields of the First World War, had lost all hope that a true and lasting peace could ever prevail in Bosnia, for this is a land of eternal hate, Max said, as he later wrote to Andrić – here people love, hate and die without ever realizing that they are walking over ground saturated in evil, he wrote; that is why I have decided to leave for ever this beautiful but terrible land, he wrote; I bid farewell to a city where people are still living each in his own time; some organize their lives by the Catholic clock, others by the Orthodox, while yet others heed only the mysterious song that comes from the tall minaret of the Bey Mosque; as for the Jews here, we have no clock of our own but God always knows what time it is, Max said, as Andrić writes; whose side should I take, whom should I believe? Max Levenfeld said; the only thing I desire is to live freely and work honestly, so I am going, I am leaving my native Sarajevo; I travel to Trieste, where my mother is again living, but then eventually I will move to South America for good, wrote Max Levenfeld, a Sarajevo Jew and Andrić's young friend, Spomenka said. Nor did the future great writer Ivo Andrić, after parting with his friend at the train station in Slavonski Brod, ever again return to Sarajevo; first, he travelled the world for many years as a diplomat and, mainly, as a cosmopolitan, artist and writer, Spomenka said; it was only with the outbreak of the Second World War that he took refuge in Belgrade, where he shut himself away in a one-room flat and, right up to the liberation, wrote his great works, Spomenka said. Andrić tells us at the end of his *Letter from 1920* that while he never again saw his young friend, he had heard that Max Levenfeld later made a name for himself as a doctor among our émigrés in Paris; he was treating them without charge for many years, and he took care of them in other ways as well. Max Levenfeld disappeared for ever on a battlefield in the Spanish Civil War, where he fought on the side of the Republicans, Andrić reports; his hospital was hit by a bomb during an air attack and he died along with most of his patients, Andrić writes. And thus died a man who was trying to escape evil, Andrić writes at the end of his *Letter*, Spomenka said when the bell sounded and the tram stopped for a moment. She got off and waved to me with the bags in her hands.

I rode on to Antwerp station.

AFTERWORD

by Stephen Watts

Panorama is Dušan Šarotar's fourth novel, following on from *Island of the Dead*, *Billiards at Hotel Dobray* and *Stay with Me, My Dear*. It was first published in Ljubljana by Beletrina in 2014 to positive reviews, and this fine English translation by Rawley Grau, published by Istros Books in association with Peter Owen as part of the Peter Owen World Series, is – running against the more usual flow for British publishers – the first into any language, although a Spanish translation is also forthcoming. It is a short, compact, complex and densely lyrical text, a meditation *inter alia* on language, time, memory, loss and love.

On the surface – and it has many surfaces, many interlocking over-layers – it tells a number of stories relating to an interlocutor, a Slovene writer who has travelled to Galway perhaps to give a reading but more to find peace and a place in which to write. He stays on and travels through the Connemara landscapes, usually in the company of Gjini, an Albanian journalist who had migrated to Galway City some many years before and who, in turn, also makes journeys around Connemara with a Canadian woman who is there in search of peace in her father's roots. Woven through these strands are many others concerning the narrator's time in a number of Belgian cities, discussions and meetings with ex-Yugoslav writers and friends he knows who work there, many of them former refugees from the wars in Bosnia and the destruction of Sarajevo, another city – in addition to Galway, Brussels, Antwerp and Ghent – that has a strong place in Šarotar's narrative. Except that *narrative* is a misleading term, or, rather, if it is the term to be used then it needs be understood in a very contemporary sense of broken weave.

In many ways it is a meditation on loss and change – 'I saw tracks in the lightly pressed grass, in the fine sand on the shore and then in the slight rippling of the water's surface; she is leaving, I thought; she is running back to the sun' – and on time, migration, language, ocean, love and war. It is densely compacted: its two hundred or so pages seem to expand much as a paper flower from childhood did when put in water, or to have the dense, burnable qualities of the peat that provides part of its subject matter and background; or as a tablet that holds immense numbers of images in its compacted layers, its clouds. The text seems able, indeed, to talk of departed days, while at the same time to be startlingly relevant to time-fractured contemporary lives. Not surprisingly, travel is a constant theme: railway journeys abound, within Belgium and even the anachronistic one from Galway to Clifden, as do bus journeys, be they from Galway, within Antwerp or from Sarajevo to Mostar, and car journeys on the wild roads of Connemara or interiors of Bosnia; but also journeys by hydrofoil; by bicycle through remote moors as also through the Belgian country-side and both to the sea's edges; and journeys negotiating cities and moorlands by foot. And cities get named almost as people: Mostar, Maribor, Antwerp, Galway, Sarajevo, Ghent, Brussels and others almost in passing. There are asides on great literature, on teaching literature, on translation, on bars and in bars (in Galway, on the Aran Islands, in Brussels), on bookshops, on empty beaches, on peat whose compression echoes the prose, on lighthouses and, above all, on migration and the wars that cause migration. Much of the middle sections of the book tilts around Ypres, Ypres of the First World War and the Ypres of today. One of the journeys outlined is that taken by the Order of the Irish Dames of Ypres from their destroyed convent in 1914 to their eventual purchase of Kylemore Castle in the raw heart of Connemara. Yet, despite the intensity and range of life strands in the narrative (let's stay with this word), Šarotar has plenty of room for lyric interlude, for lyric flights that become part of the book's texture and are earthed by the turf and architecture of land and city or pulled apart by the power of the sea.

Panorama takes as starting point the migration of an Albanian journalist and the migrations of many from the west coast of Ireland throughout the past almost two hundred years. Yet another starting point, though, is the work of Gerhard Richter, whose exhibition 'Panorama', shown in Ghent in 2008, is alluded to and seems to hover over much of the text. Šarotar is, in fact, also a photographer and film-maker: his intuitions towards Richter's sequence 'Clouds' (some of which were shown in Ghent and are echoed in Šarotar's own photographs of cloudscapes in the text) have clear reverberations right through the novel, and a Richter quote that prefaces the Ghent catalogue might really be describing part of Šarotar's probing: 'I don't mistrust reality, of which I know next to nothing,' says Richter, 'I mistrust the picture of reality conveyed to us by our senses, which is imperfect and circumscribed.' But the novel is also a paean to certain writers of the former Yugoslavia and a meditation on Balkan histories: the Slovene poet Gregor Strniša whose spirit – especially in his volume *Vesolje* (*Space*) – runs like a dark star through the text, and, above all, Ivo Andrić, whose short story 'Letter from 1920' is evoked as a spirit-level to our lives and whose own life hinges us back to the origins and outbreak of the First World War that then erupted so brutally across Europe and the tidal trope of which manages to bring this novel to its conclusion in almost elegiac calm.

And, surely, behind all this is also W.G. Sebald. His presence is sensed from the opening pages of the book, from its first sentences, and then in its final ten or so pages there it is, a grateful allusion to Sebald's *Austerlitz*, the Slovene translation of which had appeared in 2005. Šarotar had previously read *The Emigrants* in translation, and that had made a deep impression, and, at the time of writing, he is preparing an introduction to the forthcoming Slovene translation of *The Rings of Saturn*. In *Panorama* he has clearly taken Sebald into his prose-stream, into the blood of his writing: the densely layered overlapping of texts, the congested confusions of reported speech and textually rich doubt as to quite who might on occasion be speaking, the use or inclusion of photographs in the text (although Šarotar's use is subtly different from Sebald's), the occasional intended, demystifying 'error' (as in the misspelling of Guglielmo as Gugliemo from the plaque to Marconi, which intentionally is not 'corrected' in the text), the collaging of various references and sources. But there are also strong differences between the two, and if Šarotar in his novel places his work in the tradition of Sebald, it is at an angle very much his own. His *Panorama* is a development from his previous prose, in particular the short story collection *Nostalgia* and his novel *Billiards at Hotel Dobray*. This latter – an account of the persecution of Jews in Šarotar's home town of Murska Sobota in north-eastern Slovenia, close to the Hungarian border – is based on the life of his grandfather. Its prose may be less dense and compact, less 'Joycean' than that of *Panorama*. In *Panorama* Šarotar seeks to condense time until it is on the point of imploding in on itself and the reader, and here he is reminiscent of László Krasznahorkai or the latter's filmic collaborations with Béla Tarr. Train and travel are refrains throughout their work, too: the final words of Šarotar's novel, beautifully brief and laconic at the end of a text where language has been so compacted and urgent as to be almost its central character, are simply 'I rode on to Antwerp station.'